IN EVERY SENSE
LIKE LOVE

Simona Vinci was born in 1970 and lives near Bologna. Since the success of her first novel, *A Game We Play*, she has become a well-known figure in Italian cultural life and she currently presents a popular TV arts programme. She is working on her second novel.

Simona Vinci

IN EVERY SENSE
LIKE LOVE

Stories

TRANSLATED BY
Minna Proctor

VINTAGE

Published by Vintage 2002

2 4 6 8 10 9 7 5 3 1

Copyright © Simona Vinci 1999
Translation copyright © Minna Proctor 2001

Simona Vinci has asserted her right under the Copyright,
Designs and Patents Act 1988 to be identified as the author
of this work

First published in Great Britain by
Chatto & Windus 2001

Vintage
Random House, 20 Vauxhall Bridge Road,
London SW1V 2SA

Random House Australia (Pty) Limited
20 Alfred Street, Milsons Point, Sydney
New South Wales 2061, Australia

Random House New Zealand Limited
18 Poland Road, Glenfield,
Auckland 10, New Zealand

Random House (Pty) Limited
Endulini, 5A Jubilee Road, Parktown 2193,
South Africa

The Random House Group Limited Reg. No. 954009
www.randomhouse.co.uk

A CIP catalogue record for this book
is available from the British Library

ISBN 0 099 28749 8

Papers used by Random House are natural, recyclable
products made from wood grown in sustainable forests.
The manufacturing processes conform to the environ-
mental regulations of the country of origin

Printed and bound in Denmark by
Nørhaven Paperback A/S, Viborg

For Enrico,
with all the things I didn't say to him

Contents

In every sense like love   in every sense
And the hours have passed   only the hours
Had a sharp blade   which bathed
[my cheeks in blood.

Shinkawa Kazue, 'Not A Metaphor'

Black August

So much rain, so much life like the swollen sky
of this black August.

Derek Walcott, 'Dark August'

The car windows are always dirty. It's an old car and to tell the truth, it's not as if I do much to hide it.

The tyres are bald and each time we cross a water slick my arms shake with fear. The top of the car is covered with dust: sand from the beach at Corte dei Butteri where I took the girl for a few days. To walk. To collect the white shells she likes so much.

She keeps them in a yellow plastic bag among the confusion of suitcases in the back of the car. They get broken. They crumble. The bag slides back and forth and gets squashed by the heavy suitcases that roll over on to it in the morning when we pull out of the hotel car park. But my girl doesn't know that. She never looks at them after she's collected them; she never pulls them out of their yellow bag. She's already thinking about the shells she's going to collect later today, or tomorrow. When the beach is in sight she becomes restless. She tries to turn around in her seat and get the bag out of the back; but even if she reaches it, she never looks inside. She puts it on her lap and stares straight ahead. She follows the white line of the beach, eyes focused, nostrils flared like a truffle hound.

There's no sun today. It's a late August day. The kind of day there are so many of at the sea. The sky is overcast. The sea is black. The wind breaks over the surface of the water. There aren't many people at the beach. A forgotten, closed-up umbrella. Two or three folding chairs tossed on the ground. Some solitary walkers. A dog barking at the waves.

I brought her here all the same. You don't need sun to collect shells. It's good for her. She can walk barefoot on the cool sand, breathe the clean air, have a mission with her shell collection.

I glance at her now and then while I'm driving. She's quite a little girl, with long dark blond hair that she keeps in a low ponytail. Her hair always seems dirty. Like the car, like everything I'm supposed to be looking after. This occurs to me while I'm driving, my right foot pressed to the accelerator, my hand on the gearstick. Everything that belongs to me is like this: dirty, unkempt, run-down. Not just the car, the house, the garden, but my daughter too.

My little girl doesn't seem to be bothered by this though. She watches the road in front of us and thinks about her shell collection. She's fine.

We stopped for petrol this morning. The service station was a kind of island rising out of the burnt-red fields of the Maremma. All around us there were horses, moving slowly, swinging their heads and tails in the wind, making their chestnut coats ripple. There were cows and white bulls with enormous horns. My girl leaned out of the car window and called *moo moo*. The cows didn't look up from their grazing. Their eyelids were lowered to keep out the flies.

The instant we stopped at the service station she shot out of the car, leaving the door wide open behind her. A fat lady sat in front of the cashier's window. She was wearing a short dress, rolled up over her massive tanned thighs. Her lap seemed soft and strong. I would have liked to run to her and bury my head in it, feel the warmth of her skin, let her smell wash over me – a clean and healthy smell, but a little sour and salty from the heat. I watched my daughter run to the woman and stop short in front of her. Like the cows, the woman didn't lift her head, she just fanned her bosom with a rolled-up newspaper and puffed her lips.

My girl reached out for the lady's knee and touched it softly.

What a strange thing, I thought, as I watched from behind the wheel, how frightening: my daughter always does the things I want to do only a fraction of a second after I've thought of them. Even if it's a stupid thing – like most of the things of this sort that happen to us. Maybe when she's big it will be the same, but with more serious things. As if she were an extension of me, of my half-hearted life. As if she were a step toward the definite. Yes, it's more like that. My daughter does, while I've always only thought about doing. She closes the circle, completes the drawing. She takes over for me without even knowing.

The woman didn't say anything. She watched the girl without smiling and finally stood up. We bought petrol and left.

How long have we been on this journey, the clouds racing over the windscreen, the countryside stretching out in every direction through the car windows? A few days, perhaps a week. The hotels look alike. The bed-and-breakfasts look alike. Only in my head, because in reality, they are different from one another. In my head, the images get confused – corners and ceilings, curtains, tables and beds. If I think about them, they scramble and recompose themselves like the fragments in a kaleidoscope – the kind I liked when I was little and now you can't find any more – forming non-existent bedrooms in which a shell-shaped soap dish from the hotel in Capalbio is sitting on the chipped walnut desk from the seafront B&B in Principina.

The same thing sometimes happens with people's faces and words. They get mixed up and you can't remember who said what when. It's better not to think about it. I forget these things when I'm driving. But the details stick.

When I first go into a room, I try to get a visual impression of it in a single stroke, but I can never do it. Inevitably my eyes fall on some insignificant detail and that cancels out the impression of the whole. The room disappears. Nothing's left but the horizontal stripe on the curtain, the dark varnish on the desk, a tear in the bedspread, the tree growing against the window – a dry branch reaching out towards me like an old lady's arm.

The girl doesn't look at anything. She comes into the room quickly, her steps efficient and sturdy – a little like a farmer, it's something she inherited from her father. She throws the yellow bag on to the side of the bed that she's chosen as her side – usually the side closest to the window – and she sits down on the floor to take off her shoes. She wears big black and white trainers with thick soles and bright laces all knotted up. She always looks straight ahead and she doesn't say anything.

I know she's hungry but I want her to tell me. Instead she waits. She's waiting for me to decide that it's time to think about dinner. I take a shower and spread moisturising creams and lotions over me, listening to the metronomic beat of her ping-pong ball against the wall.

Although earlier today, in the car, she did tell me she was hungry. She didn't turn her head or change expression.

I'm hungry.

I slowed down to look at her, then I went back to normal speed, actually, I sped up, hoping a snack bar or a restaurant, anything, might appear on the horizon.

After the event at the petrol station, she fell into an even deeper silence than usual. Her hands lay still on her knees, the seat belt fastened across her chest, her lips tight. The yellow bag was at her feet, sealed shut.

Today at the beach she didn't collect shells. She stood on the shore, toes buried into the cool sand, hands curled into tight fists at her side, and watched the still pale line of the sea.

Some days I get tired. Some days, I get tired of it all, the car, the child, this ridiculous trip that's been going on for too long, this horrible August with its dark clouds and heavy sense of dissolution. I would like to take my little girl by her shoulders and shake her, force her to get out of the car, and plant her somewhere in the middle of the Maremma. I'd leave her there like you leave a suitcase that's just become extra weight. I'm sure nothing would happen to her. She'd stay there as still as a rock, become a part of the nature. A stone, a dead tree trunk, a clump of red earth, fertile and mute. Maybe she'd put down roots. She'd turn into a tree, a thick bush.

In front of us: the road carved into the red earth. Beside us: more red earth, white cows, horses and shrubs.

The car cuts through the middle of this Wild West landscape, where every so often a little train passes. It looks like where I come from, the northern plains, but the colours are more vibrant here.

In the middle of a field: three old rusting bathtubs.

On the beach: I watch the opaque water break over the black rocks. Black, shiny rocks; they look volcanic. The rain comes down faster, at a slant now. The little circles in the puddles between the rocks disappear suddenly, sucked back into the waves.

I imagine my child slipping on the rocks, the soft rubber of her trainers sliding across the wet surface. I see her little head break open like a melon on the sharp edge of a black rock. The blood that pours out, the brain matter. A ripe fruit cracked open and dripping juice.

Strangely, my thoughts don't upset me; they calm me. I see her slender body carried off by the dark waves and all the traces of her blood washed away by the sea. Then back to the black rocks, shiny in the intense early-afternoon light. The silence after the downpour, with only the sound of the waves in the crevices between the rocks.

It isn't the first time this sort of thing has happened to me. Especially over these last few days. It happened at the top of the steps leading to the beach, where there's a view of the Madonna of the Sea. I imagined her falling down, rolling like a bolt of fabric, a bedspread, a carpet. Without a sound, or even a groan. Just disappearing over the top of the last step.

Now, back in the car, the windows down and the wind whistling in, I sneak a look and I think that I love her. No matter what, I can't stop. Her squashed profile, dirty hair, the way her lip juts out, and the yellow bag on her lap. She's there. She's proof, the only proof, of my life. We're together on this road, slick now with rain.

I take the exit for Talamone. I'm holding the wheel tight with both hands and I follow the curves, leaning my whole body and my head to the side.

We could crash. I could lose control of the car and let it skid across the water. We could hit the wall, perhaps scraping along it first for a few metres, the sparks flying off the door like so many beautiful lights, until the car bounced against it one final time and exploded in a single, sudden burst. My little girl's hair would be the first thing to burn. Like a bundle of yellow hay, a rolled-up beach mat, a straw broom. A hungry, blue flame.

We stop along the way at a dirty little hotel, more of a motel. We park the car behind the tiny red brick building where, with a vague sweep of her arm, the owner had told us to leave it.

Two nut-coloured dogs are racing back and forth between the parked cars. My girl isn't interested in dogs. While I unload the suitcases and the big bag with the towels she kicks at the red dirt, watching the clouds of dust rise up from the soles of her shoes. The dogs run towards her. Without looking at them, my daughter kicks a couple of times in their direction, hitting them with the dirt. They yelp and run to hide under the hot belly of a parked car. Crouching there in the dusty shade, they watch the girl's feet, stubbornly digging into the dirt and kicking up clouds.

The room is decent. There's a little window that looks out over the fields; a row of thin, crooked olive trees queues drunkenly up the hill and vanishes from sight. The clouds through the window are large and dark. Steel grey. It will start raining again soon. I watch the field through the window. My girl is sitting at the bottom of the row of olive trees, playing with the red dirt. The dogs keep their distance, but they are watching her, sniffing the air. She suddenly gets to her feet and starts running. She runs up the hill following the row of olive trees. She's awkward when she runs. Her arms pump back and forth, and she keeps her head lowered like a mule. When she gets to the top, she stops suddenly and lifts her palms up to the sky. Then she lets them fall back down to her side.

My girl does strange things. But I know that. I'm used to it.

Late in the day, after we've taken a nap on the hard narrow motel bed, we get in the car and go to the beach at Alberese. This late in the day there's only a slender stretch of sand left, the rest has been swallowed by the sea.

As usual, I watch from a distance. I watch her walk on the shore, her thin legs sticking out of her blue Bermuda shorts, her feet bare, her shoes abandoned somewhere between me and sea, the yellow plastic bag held tightly in her hand. She doesn't turn to look at me even once. She paces back and forth along a path of her own choosing, from a dried-up piece of driftwood to a flame-orange umbrella. She hasn't yet collected a single shell. She just looks at the horizon and walks.

And what if the sea took her? I think. This sea, something out of a romantic painting, waves whipped by the wind and tinged green and white, what if this sea were to close over her head? A soft wave, just a little taller, whirling and warm, could drag her in and swallow her up.

There wouldn't be any need for a funeral, for a white coffin lowered into the earth. Her body would float among the fish, dissolve in the pure water, become a single pale worm, a tadpole, something like the beginning of life.

My little girl turns around. She puts her shoes back on without brushing off the sand from between her toes. She didn't collect anything today. The yellow bag stayed closed.

These thoughts I have are like the rustling of wind through leaves. The gentle swaying of birch-tree leaves, like small coins. They are the strange shape that love takes on certain days. And then they disappear as soon as I've thought them, leaving me feeling naked and clean once more, the shadows gone. For a while I can't even remember all the irritations of being pregnant. The enormous stomach, the spots on my face, the nausea, the heaviness in my legs. I can't remember the pain I felt the day she was born, or how annoyed it makes me to trip over muddy trainers left out in the middle of the pale wall-to-wall carpeting we have at home.

It's raining again today. It's August rain, black and angry, rain that tinkles its way out to sea, leaving only a haze on the horizon.

We're on the beach but we are not alone. There's a couple moving towards us through the blue and white water. They walk slowly, pushing their legs against the heavy resistance of the current. He's waist-deep in the water. The woman seems much younger. She's wearing an old-fashioned hat with a wide brim. It's white and held down by a yellow and blue polka-dot scarf. She wears a dark one-piece swimsuit. She's slender and elegant, her face lightly marked by a delicate web of wrinkles. The man has white hair and is stooped. There's sickness on his face. He holds the woman as he walks and occasionally mutters something. When they get closer I realise that the woman is helping him exercise.

Come on. Let go. Don't be so stiff. Relax your muscles. Come on. I'll hold you. Not like that. Not like that . . .

Her voice is calm.

That's enough. I'm done now. Let me get out. I'm tired. That's enough, I'm telling you . . .

She holds him with both arms. His face is buried in her neck. She holds him up and slowly drags him towards the shore.

Even my little girl has stopped to watch them, her eyes neutral, her skin covered in goose bumps. Her bare feet are buried in the wet sand by the water. She's holding the yellow bag tightly.

What is she seeing?

I watch her and I watch the couple as they move off in the same direction they came from.

My girl isn't hungry this evening. She plays with her food, pushing the pasta and meat sauce around the oval plate. She looks out of the restaurant window at the dark pine trees. The two dogs are asleep on the ground, their noses squashed into the red dirt.

Before bed, already in her pyjamas, she asks if she can go outside. No, she can't. It's time for bed. Tomorrow.

The next day on the beach she doesn't take her trainers off and walks far away holding her yellow bag tight against her chest. She comes to a big tree, black as if it has been burned, and stops. She opens the bag and looks inside. She sees the pieces of shell, all that white dust. Razor-like shards, white and grey, some blue and pink. Without looking, she dumps the entire contents out on to the sand. She shakes the bag a little and then lets that drop too. The wind carries it away immediately. A slightly stronger gust fills it and makes it fly like a balloon.

My little girl turns around towards me, her face calm and blank like a sheet of paper.

The rain has stopped. The circles on the water disappear and a diffuse orange light rises over the water, as if it were coming out of the sea, bursting through the surface. It's September advancing. This black August is over.

The strange direction that love takes on certain days.

The Courtyard

Do individual loves exist? I think not. Love is an atmospheric solution, it's potassium and iodine, it's delirium.

Alda Merini, 'The Torment of Shapes'

I live in a working–class neighbourhood. It's a long bus ride to get anywhere near my street and the view changes in a flash from one stop to the next. The vehicle rounds a corner, and the view is different, it's become somewhere else.

The city centre is medieval red stone, but the further you get from the centre, the more it all turns into sprawl just like any other sprawl: shopping complexes, bigger and bigger billboards, sad, empty little gardens, blocks of flats. Dirty streets. Black dust.

Seen from the outside, the houses in my street seem almost pretty. Even though old and crumbling, the façades are attractive. People who end up here by accident look around surprised but impressed.

But they have never been through the gates; they've never seen the courtyards on the inside.

My apartment has a little balcony over the courtyard. The railing is painted green, a very pale green, the colour of new grass. Climbing ivy, geraniums and branches thick with tiny leaves extend out into the emptiness and hang there, shifting in the wind and rain.

There's a terracotta sun hanging over the screen door. My father gave it to me a long time ago when he was still around. Now he lives in another city. Sometimes, without warning, he visits. It happens once a year. He crosses the courtyard and heads to my door and I sit and watch him from the window. I look at his dark skin, lined with wrinkles that are deeper every time I see him. That's my father. I repeat it to myself a thousand times so I won't forget. My father.

I'm on holiday. I sit here for hours watching the builders working on the house next door. I like their filthy clothes speckled with cement, their hard and callused hands. Their banter and cigarette smoke. The old-fashioned gestures they make.

I like the smell of poverty, of lost youth, the smell of mud and wet sand.

This courtyard has always been the same. As long as I can remember the silence has been absolute. Sounds come in from the outside, from the street – cars and trucks passing by, street cleaners, buses – but nothing ever happens here on the inside. There are no children playing, no women talking. Everyone is shut inside their own apartment, windows closed, curtains drawn. They have learned not to be ashamed of the musty smell of crumbling walls, a smell that gets into your clothes and under your skin and stays there, but they still shut their doors. People greet each other hurriedly, without a smile; hands tucked into pockets so that they don't have to offer them. It's the dignity of poverty. Total and extreme.

The branches of the trees intertwine and form a black shield over the whole courtyard – an armour of leaves that blocks out the sun. Only a few thin blades of light are able to slice through. A barely perceptible shift in the foliage above makes it completely dark below. I sit here. My eyes open, my hands abandoned in my lap, my body offered up to the light, to the motion of the day.

There's a man who passes by every evening.

He's methodical; he always comes at exactly the same time, just a little after seven. He walks slowly back and forth along the road.

Maybe he lives in one of these houses, I don't know. I've never seen him going into or coming out of a doorway. He's out on the street and he walks. Sometimes he has a dog with him; more often he doesn't. He pauses in front of our gate and looks inside. He looks into the dark courtyard at the dense trees, the closed windows. He stands there for a long time. He doesn't see me watching him. His expression is pained. It hurts me to look at him. His eyes stand out and he has deep lines at the corners of his mouth. I watch him every evening. He doesn't know this. One time I think of calling to him, waving, but what would I say.

But if I were to say something, say anything, he'd surely lift his head and see me. He'd wake from his daze and go somewhere else, to a quieter place where he can be just looking again.

Because it's clear that he's not looking at anything in particular. He's not looking for anything here, he's not looking for anything in particular anywhere. It's only that this courtyard makes him want to look.

I call to him. I've decided to do it. I call out. Though, as I'm doing it, I'm no longer sure why I decided to shout instead of saying something.

Now, out on the street, there's a man looking in at me.

Now that he's here, standing in front of me, waiting for me to say something, or at least make some kind of gesture, I'm suddenly indifferent to his presence.

I desired it utterly, and now I don't. I don't care at all. He's ugly, old, wrinkled. It's impossible I ever needed him. I was fine alone. The evening was cool, quiet. His presence is totally useless.

I look at his white canvas shoes, his pale suit which is too light for this season.

I feel obliged to talk, to say something.

I always see you standing there . . . I thought that you might be waiting for something . . . I don't know why.

I'm here a lot . . . Maybe it's the colour of this courtyard, the leaves on the trees, the smell most of all . . . I never know where to go at night. Going home is too hard, so I try to use up the time, to walk a little . . .

Maybe I should ask him why, but I don't feel like it. It doesn't occur to me.

He's got a low slippery voice; he drags out all the syllables.

He looks at my hands, lips, breasts. One piece of me at a time, as if I weren't a whole body but chunks cut up and displayed in a row on a butcher's counter. He keeps doing it.

Will you offer me a drink?

I should answer him, or send him away. It wasn't an invitation, my cry. But it's obvious what he's thinking. What he's thinking I want.

He might be right. I look at him. Maybe I've desired him since the first time I saw him. But I didn't know it.

He smiles and looks at me whole.

Do you always look at people like that?

Why? How am I looking at you? He laughs.

First the details then the whole.

It's possible. I've never noticed.

I reach up towards his grey hair. Sticky waves falling through my fingers.

You should go now. My brother's coming back and I have to get dinner ready. I have to change clothes, please . . .

Why do you need to change? That dress looks good on you.

Please, I think, *go away*.

He goes away. I watch him disappear through the gate. He doesn't look up once.

It's only six o'clock and the man is already in the street. Walking back and forth. Without looking up. He keeps his hands in his pockets. He has the same suit and shoes on as yesterday. He doesn't stop walking. His footsteps echo through the courtyard. He only raises his eyes once but then he doesn't lower them again.

There were no words.

The bare room is completely white: walls, tiles, sheets. Cold and white like a monastic cell, or a prison.

He undressed quickly, using the same simple movements he must use when he gets undressed alone at night before going to bed. He kept his eyes lowered, looking at his fly, his shirt buttons, cuffs, the dirty laces of his canvas shoes.

I decided to undress the same way, without malice. I was like a novice, seated on a virgin's narrow cot, legs together, back straight. I took off my shirt, my skirt, my tights. I kept my underwear on and waited to see what he did. He took his off, just as he'd taken off his clothes. His pale body stirred no desire in me. It was an ordinary body. I felt as if I were watching, without being seen, a stranger take off his clothes to get into a bath or a shower. There was no hair on his body, or muscle; it was all sluggish flesh – too white. For a moment, my hands remembered other bodies.

I removed the remainder of my clothing. My breasts bobbed when I leaned over to pull down my knickers. But he wasn't watching. He came close to me with his eyes shut and pulled me to him in such an intimate way it seemed we were an old married couple. As if we both knew all the movements, as if we'd already repeated them thousands of times. Over and over, for innumerable days and nights.

My hands are lazy on his body, indifferent to the curves and dips. They're distracted hands.

My hair crackles under his dry palms. Little black fires.

We sit in silence, on the edge of everything: we have no pity, emotions, love.

It's been six months since I've touched anyone's body but my own. And still I feel nothing. Though I should because one learns new things from every lover – nuances, movements. Not words. No. All the words have been repeated hundreds of times to different men.

I speak a mute language.

We're in bright light. I'm not frightened. His open eyes see every mark, every imperfection, each tiny crevice in my skin, which is starting to not be young any more.

Brutal and true. The light performs its violent work, stripping us of the warm hue that darkness wraps around bodies.

I'm irritated by his hot skin and his ragged, sharp fingernails.

My eyes follow the shadows on the walls, the cracks in the ceiling. The room is too cold. Who knows if he even remembers that it's me on him.

Is he the one I've been waiting for? The free and happy one I imagined, the one who would bring no wounds or tears, no scars, the one who would spread open my legs quickly without asking me anything.

But he isn't like that. Sure, he didn't ask me anything. But he is neither free, nor happy.

Afterwards, we walk in the courtyard. He wears his rumpled pastel suit, and I'm in a red bathrobe.

The black leaves rustle above our heads. The moon must be behind them.

My brother comes home, opens the window, and calls me. He says, Are you hungry? Are either of you hungry?

We say yes. He shuts the window.

The light glows pale behind the glass. I see the shadow of his movements: he gets out plates and glasses and sets them on the table, he turns on the gas under the white enamel pot. He runs his hand through his soft hair, he closes his tired eyes.

I see him leave the kitchen and go into the room where we sleep together. He makes the bed, still rumpled and damp from our bodies. This doesn't bother him. Nothing bothers him.

We continue to walk round the courtyard. The humidity digs its claws into your bones. I tighten the red bathrobe around me. Over us and around us, there are so many lit windows.

He turns his head up towards the branches; his mouth half open as if waiting to receive a drop of water from the sky.

I tighten my arms around me, feeling my skin through the stiff towelling of the bathrobe.

We could lie down on the black ground and shut our eyes. We could listen to the sound of earthworms below us. Sleep on the ground. In this sad courtyard that's given birth to my love. Because it's clear that this is what love is. What else could it be?

I don't know his name and I don't think I want to know. Some syllable that stands for him but isn't him.

Words take away, they transport, they alter your perception. I've known that since I was a child and absolutely refused to learn to read or write. When I turned the pages of books and let the mysterious black characters flow before my eyes, I'd suddenly feel that it wouldn't take more than a few moments for the confusion of marks to arrange themselves and make clear sense in my mind – and I'd slam the book shut, my heart in my throat. I had escaped. I knew that once things acquire meaning, they no longer astonish you, and you're lost.

Blessed are the poor in spirit, for theirs is the kingdom of heaven. Blessed are the meek, for they shall inherit the earth. And I – I wanted to stay simple. To experience wonder.

The same wonder I feel now, here in this dark courtyard buried in mud and dust, the leaves moving over my head.

I walk, letting my bare feet get dirty with mud, letting them sink into the soft ground. He walks with me. Silently brushing my arm with his jacket sleeve.

I know he's one of those men who don't know love's words. He made love with his eyes shut, and didn't make a sound. I kept my eyes open. I would have liked to talk, but you don't talk to someone who's not going to answer. That's what my father always told me when I was little. I never talked and so he told me, I'm not going to talk to you either . . . I'm never speaking to you again . . . Then you'll see . . .

It's better this way. Words steal the spirit. They blow it out into the wind and confusion. Then they destroy it.

He takes a pack of cigarettes from his jacket pocket. I don't see the brand, but they smell strong. He doesn't offer me one, not even a puff. He smokes quickly, sucking the filter, chewing it between his teeth. You can see he's a heavy smoker. I could already tell that from his breath, from how the nails on his right hand were disgustingly yellow with nicotine.

I don't think there is one thing I like about him. And that's why I love him. It may seem an absurd contradiction, but it's true.

Love without object is vertigo.

Like faith. Who has ever seen the face of God?

Loving what disgusts you, the horrible, the deformed, the sick, is even stronger.

It's height without measure and you can feel it moving inside you.

Like when I was little and I'd reach out and touch the boy next to me at school, touch his destroyed skin. He had a burn that wrapped itself around his head and chest – a mask of flesh, fused into whatever must have been there before.

None of the other children wanted to sit next to him, so I sat there. And sometimes I'd touch him. Let my fingertips slide across the ridges of his cooked flesh. It was strangely cool, and the horror of that first moment became vertigo, and then love.

I don't know what this man is like. Whether he's ugly or not. I watch him under the bright light of the almost full moon, the shadows of the leaves passing over his forehead and cheeks.

He has a straight nose, too big to be nice. His mouth is thin and wet. His forehead is marked with deep lines; his skin is covered with little holes. His eyes are big and languid, expressionless. His eyebrows are thick and wiry, his hair is grey and sparse with patches of pink scalp showing through it. I look at the details, then I widen my gaze to get perspective and he goes out of focus.

I don't know what he's like. I can't seem to decide.

The way his shoulders slope makes my heart ache.

I love him.

My brother calls us from the window.

It's ready, are you coming up?

Yes, we're coming.

We hold hands as we climb the stairs.

What will my brother say about him? What will he think? And what could I tell him? We'll stay silent. He doesn't trust words either. We were born of the same father.

The table is set simply, without pretension: plates, cutlery, bread basket and a paper tablecloth. There's boiling hot vegetable soup in the pot. A plate of cold meat and salad. I never ask for anything when he cooks. I like it all. I like that it comes from his hands.

The man who two hours ago was in our bed is now seated across from my brother and has his head bowed over his plate. He should be in some other house at this hour, maybe with someone, a wife, a child. Instead, he's here, sitting in silence and blowing on his spoon to cool down the soup.

Do you sleep together?

He says it suddenly, lifting his head.

My brother doesn't answer. He looks at me, wanting me to be the one to speak.

Yes.

I can't offer him any explanation. Yes is all that comes to mind.

We're both alone. We keep each other company. I listen to his breath at night, and it's as if it were mine, echoed. A sweet, twin breath.

But he doesn't ask any more questions; it doesn't seem to interest him.

He doesn't know about the other men, who, just like him, sat at this same table and ate in silence under the sad light of this orange lamp. He doesn't know that others, like him, made love to me in that bed, and that I loved them with this same vertiginous love.

After dinner, my brother Lucio clears the table. We sit and watch him. We're like two tired children, eyelids drooping and bellies full of food, but still wanting something. The evening isn't over yet; it's still not time to go to sleep in the dark, to suffocate under the covers.

He lights a cigarette and blows smoke into the air. Grey-blue clouds, like the fur of Persian cats, clouds shaped like mouths and feet. I look at them through lowered eyes; I watch how they disappear, sliding through the open window.

Lucio shakes the tablecloth into the courtyard, leaning out over the balcony. He washes the plates without making any clinking noises; all we hear is water flowing into the sink and the popping of soap bubbles.

Afterwards, his hands are red and swollen. He rests them on the table and leans towards us without looking us in the eyes.

Would you like a whisky?

Why not, he says.

Why not. How I like that expression. I could repeat it a thousand times a day, every time someone asks me a question, every time I have to decide whether or not to do something. Why not. Why not. It's open. Anything is possible.

I follow my brother's hands as he collects the glasses and the bottle. He sets everything on the table. His movements are slow. His fingers move like big, stiff caterpillars. Then I look at the hands of the man next to me. His hands are smooth, delicate. Hands that don't know how to grab, only how to touch. I already know this. I look at the nicotine yellow on the fingers of his right hand, pale stains like on a tablecloth that hasn't been washed properly. Signs that tell stories. Confused scenes, barely articulated but true. They are his hands, his habits, his life.

These are stories I don't want to hear, places I don't want to see.

I listen to the sound of lips – my brother's lips, and the man's lips – the way they part to let the liquid slide into their mouths. How their tongues rest for an instant on the palate, then come down again, to run over the teeth.

There are no other sounds. The room is sweet, lit by a warm, gentle light. There's just a slight breeze coming in through the open window. The whisper of leaves in the courtyard. There are no televisions or radios on. There's not even the sound of voices.

I wrap the silence around me as if it were a soft blanket. I roll myself into it, eyes closed, fists tight. The more I listen, the fainter the sounds become – balls of black dust disintegrating in the wind. I fall asleep, like when I was a child, a time that you can only remember as jumbled sensations – all of them physical. The body remembers things – love, people, time – better than the spirit. It carries everything inside it. The body's memory resists all storms. It's tenacious the way trees and rocks are.

My mother was this silence; she was this soft warm blanket, the breeze coming in the window, the black night stretching across the courtyard.

I fall asleep with my eyes full of black. The black sky, the black dirt.

My brother will put me to bed. He'll gather me in his arms and carry me effortlessly.

I won't open my eyes again tonight. I'll sleep in the silence of the house, in the cool wind that comes from far away and sweeps through the city and its streets.

Stretched out on the old white bed, like something fragile washed up by the tide. A shell or a scrap of wood; a cuttlefish bone, flat and hard; a tin can tossed into the waves and carried back to land.

I'll sleep and the sea will clean me. The silence will polish me like a stone; it will make me become more beautiful.

My brother will be the one to deal with him. The man who slept with me on this very bed. The man who gave me his body. His soft tongue. His sex. His smooth hands. Who entered me, mined me, then left, left me open like an empty oyster. Now I close. Silence rises from the courtyard, cloaked in darkness, it holds me and repairs me. I sleep. But before sinking, I listen to the sound of my brother's hand coming to rest on the man's body in a clumsy embrace. Who knows if he wants it. Who knows if he won't be frightened by it. My brother's body is my twin. I'm female, he's male. But we have the same bones, the same skin, the same muscles. The same black eyes. Let yourself be taken, I think, don't be scared. Listen to the sweet twin breath of our bodies intertwined with the silence around you. Others have done it. Others that I loved with the same vertiginous love.

Others whom I stopped loving.

Who now flutter lightly along with the dry leaves down in the courtyard.

All Alone

This is the room: four walls and six beds. Two tall windows that look out over the hospital car park. The car roofs are sardine tins, shiny and packed tightly next to each other, immobile in perfect rows. A car leaves, there's a hole, and another car comes to fill it. There are never any empty spaces.

Four walls, six beds, two tall windows, one door and six people lying between white sheets. The walls all match, so do the beds; the people don't, not at all. Every so often someone leaves and doesn't come back. Cured. Or, disappeared.

From my bed I can see the top of the Christmas tree that has been decorated for the patients and their friends and relatives. A kind of funereal monument, gigantic and luminous. They've put up a tree in my ward, too, at the reception desk where all the doctors and nurses gather to review patient records. It's scrawny and squashed like Charlie Brown's Christmas tree in the saddest story I've ever read. On a bench underneath the tree, they've put out cakes and wine.

There's a window right over the tree, and through that window you can see the peculiar geometry of the hospital walls: extending out, almost at a diagonal. The sky presses down on them – a grey rectangle.

When it gets dark the street under my window pulses with light, movement and sound.

The ambulance sirens and the groaning elevators, along with the footsteps of nurses and the tinkling of coins being pushed through the slots in the vending machine, and dropping.

It's the world, continuing on.

I've been in here for almost four months. It was September when I arrived and still hot out, the sky was still blue. It reminded me of when I was little. My bedroom window faced west. The sunsets filled the fields with orange waves and the sky above was a deep, saturated blue. It looked like giant flames were exploding over the tops of the trees.

The sky is not so blue any more. It tends to white in the morning, a cold and opaque white, like the ice coating that forms inside the freezer. At night it's dark blue, icy blue and starless.

I don't know my body any more. It's a foreign object over which I have no control.

I've stopped asking myself questions.

The doctors put tubes in my veins and down my throat, they tap my muscles, arrange my arms and legs. I can't feel anything. I let their hands troll my body. They cross it and plough it with their cold quick fingers; they measure it. It's all in working order, but they keep on studying me, trying to learn the virus's path, trying to follow it. I'm the one who's forgotten I have a body. I listen to their conversations floating over me: confusion that just adds to the confusion that's already invaded my brain. Too many memories, too many things grinding together – images I must hurry to collect, hold on to before they disappear for ever. Like cloud-watching: you need to pay attention in order to capture the shapes, because a second passes and there's already a new formation. Sickness is the same way. It's in constant motion. Colds, respiratory problems, rashes; each manifestation derails the last and turns into another, day after day.

I've counted the planes passing over this window; I've counted the hours, the wind's whistles; I've counted the visits of my friends and relatives. I've counted all the women I've ever met, the ones I kissed, the ones I made love to. I've tried to recall the lyrics of every song I learned when I was a child, and all the cartoons, and the action-figure collections that I started but never finished, and the names of the places I've been in my travels.

I feel the need to count everything, divide the events and people by type and sub-type, to classify them. I seem to be able to hold on to life like this; I seem to be able to assert my right to existence.

Because I'm disappearing.

I'm twenty-eight years old and I'm disappearing and everyone around me has already started getting used to the idea.

And then there are all those things I can't count because they haven't happened yet. I haven't got married, I haven't had children, and I've worked at the same job since I got my degree two years ago.

By now the difference between what's been and what might have been is no longer important. What counts is what I am: a battleground. Two armies fight over me. I'm a sci-fi movie; I'm an action movie projected on to the interior walls of a human body.

Then, there's that girl.

When I was back home, I would listen to her talk on the telephone. In summer, windows were open and voices would rise from the houses, slither down the street and drift into other houses. I'd see her shadow move on the wall and I'd imagine the expression on her face when she said *No* to one of the many men who called her.

I would have called her too if I could have. I would have. Really.

But I shouldn't say that. I need to be careful and think about other people and worry about the risk of contagion.

My mother brought me a bag of oranges today. You always give oranges to sick people. I ate all of them. There must have been ten, twelve oranges. I peeled them methodically, patiently, letting the juice drip on to my sheets and pyjamas. Stains formed, pale, pink, sticky, intersecting stains, like blood. I piled the rinds up one on top of the other, a tower of orange peels.

I stared at my tower until the nurse on duty decided to throw it out. And along with it, she took away my mother's gift, and the sun that peeked through the tower.

But at least I didn't have to watch them rot, wrinkle, and get hard and dry.

I still think of that girl.

There are a lot of women even here in the hospital. Doctors, nurses, patients, visitors: I'm not interested in them.

I've seen her make love to another man. She's the one I see every time I close my eyes, she comes to me in the dark, naked.

It was one night in June and I was out on the balcony chain-smoking because I couldn't sleep. I saw a car parked under my window next to a big tree. I didn't recognise the car; it didn't belong to any of the neighbours. It was late, three o'clock maybe. I could see shadows moving inside the car and then I heard voices. I went out so I could see better. She was on top of him, straddling him. Her dress was rolled up over her hips and there was this beautiful round arse, pale as the moon, right in my face. His hands were slowly running up and down her back. Their voices, which started as whispers, had become moans, modulating and rhythmic. I stopped watching before they had finished. I went back into the house and tried to find something to do, read a magazine, watch television. Something, anything. I wanted to go down and yank her from the car, tell her that I was there, that I was on my balcony smoking cigarettes and watching the sky. Me – trying not to think of anything; me – who would never have anyone again. Me – I had a right not to see and I had a right to be left in peace. Then she rushed out of the car and disappeared into her house.

Even here in the hospital, with tubes in my throat, an IV in my arm, hooked up to containers of dripping saline, I have the urge. When it comes, I look at the sheet rising over my erection and I look down at my hands which are covered with holes because there's no place left in my arms to put the IV. I look at the other patients lying on nearby beds. After all the looking, it passes. I stay still, waiting for my blood to flow, waiting for my body to remember where it is and what it's waiting for.

I think of the virus in order to distract myself. I like the idea of my silent virus. It's fierce, swift, sinuous. I imagine weirdly shaped micro-organisms, labouring away in a frenetic mission of destruction. They corrode the cellular membranes and when they have dissolved they enter the nucleus. It happens in silence: the organism's reaction, the antibodies triggered in attempted defence.

A diseased body is a body that's alive. The mechanics of the vital process are interrupted, redirected towards infinite redefinition. It's a constantly creative process.

Today's been a long day. I've had five or six erections. Even the nurse saw when she came to change my IV. I could see her eyes race towards the swelling under the sheet and then slither away again just as quickly.

I wasn't embarrassed. I figure that it's probably normal for her, it must be. Or maybe not. There are children, the elderly, people who just don't respond to stimulation. I'm something else. Something different from everyone else.

I have written her a letter.

I've always liked writing letters. Words are a violent courtship. They get into the flesh of whoever's reading them.

Written words are frightening.

I've always thought that when you write, it follows the rhythm of the spirit. You lie when you speak, but not when you write. It's not possible. Writing is like extracting something living and terrifying, like a vital organ squashed on to a sheet of a paper.

Wrap up a kidney and send it; this is letter-writing.

I don't remember exactly what I wrote. I know I wanted to tell her something. I wanted her to feel my words, to enter them in a single stroke. To slide quickly and surely into the centre. Right into me. I wrote about the window, my balcony that looks out over her house. That I've been in her life for a long time now, and I know she likes to listen to music in the dark with the windows open. And I know she likes South American music, like the tango or the habanera, which seems strange to me, because she's so slender and delicate she should be listening to Celtic music or some impalpable free-form Northern jazz. Instead she listens to Piazzolla in the dark. And Madredeus – but the Portuguese spirit is at least closer to her complexion, which is olive but pale as if she were sick.

I wrote that I was dying. I wrote that every day I wake up with less time, but that's true for everyone and it doesn't frighten me.

Maybe she'll come. I wrote and told her where I am, in this hospital and that if she wants, when she wants, she can come visit me, even if she doesn't want to talk about the letter, or about anything. She can sit with me for a while, and that's enough.

Time has passed. The way time passes in the hospital: slowly. I'm a snail in a shell. I'm protected by the walls, by the white coats of doctors and nurses, by the voices that never entirely quieten down. Protected by the shared suffering that makes infants of us all, makes us vulnerable to each other. Some people look for this their whole lives, making mistakes and getting sidetracked, changing houses, cities, lovers. This is a refuge. This is place where no one asks you to be anything but what you are, or to prove you know how to do things, to walk around on your tiptoes so that you'll be just a hair taller than the others. We're all equal. Real children, fake children, it doesn't matter. We're all the same age; we're all in the same bed, white and grey with a hard mattress and new sheets. The same white trays and plastic containers in front of us at dinner time. The contents change sometimes, but not always. We peek over at our neighbour's tray to make sure the orderly hasn't played a trick and given us stewed apple instead of the low-fat crème caramel everyone else got. The nurses rub our foreheads with their fingertips when we're feeling very sick or when we have a fever. They whisper that we should drink all the medicine and get some rest because tomorrow will be better. They pick up the sheet that fell to the floor and walk briskly up and down the corridor. We fall asleep to the familiar, sweet sound of their rubber soles.

Sometimes the doctors scold us. They are grumpy fathers who don't smile often, but they are fathers. This place is the house I've always wanted. With regular hours that never change, with lots of windows to look out of, and lunch and dinner served. There's a television in front of my bed, a reserve supply of sweets in the cabinet next to my bed. There are so many kind voices for me. I get camomile tea in the evening and black tea in the morning. I know that tomorrow I won't have to worry about office politics, I won't have to figure out what to do. Just like when I was little. I can stay in bed and calmly watch the day speed by.

But.

But I didn't choose this.

That's the only thing missing from all this. Choice.

Not the unforeseen. That's what I do have.

I could be a stiff by tonight. Or tomorrow. Who knows.

In the meantime, I bring hot plastic cups full of orange-spice tea sweetened with acacia honey to my lips, and the liquid soothes my throat.

In the meantime, I write letters.
And I wait.

I wrote letters, I made days and nights pass. And I waited. I waited without conviction, or delusion, without imagining the moment when her shadow would darken the doorway and she would come to me, a pack of letters clutched in her hands. I didn't try to imagine her eyes moving from my face to the clipboard at the foot of the bed, making sure it was really me.

But when she did cross my threshold, letters clutched in her hands, and her eyes restlessly shifting from my face to the clipboard and back and forth again, I was sure that the whole scene was a part of me that had always been there.

She was taller than I remembered her, and prettier, too. Her hair fell to her shoulders. She wore it loose and it was dark, but not shiny.

She stared at me but didn't speak. I tried to smile at her, but was scared of cracking something. I wanted her to take the initiative. I was happy. I was like a child lying in bed early on Christmas morning listening through the bedroom door to Santa Claus's muffled footsteps as he drags along his big sack of presents.

She sat down next to me. In silence. It was five o'clock in the afternoon and already dark. It was cold outside; I could see that from her reddened cheeks, and the tip of her nose and her chapped lips.

Seven letters are a lot for ten days.
I smiled.
Will you get me some water from the stand, please.
She reached out for the glass, then paused.
You know, I remember you. But you were different.
She flushed. She lowered her eyes and she wanted to apologise, I know she did. But she didn't. She was good. She reached out for the glass and took it. Her soft, red, cold fingers wrapped around the glass and then all of it, fingers and glass, was moving towards me. I would have liked to touch her. I would have liked to drink her

hand along with the water, let it slide down into me and massage my oesophagus.

I drank with little sips and watched her restive eyes. She couldn't decide whether to act happy or sad. The light in the room grew steadily fainter and chillier and you could hear voices in the corridor, the voices of people passing, and from the television.

I'm sorry this is such a sad place.

She smiled finally.

It's not important, you know, if you're saying that on my account.

Time passed slowly and we didn't know how to be. Then I took her hand without thinking about it. I rested my whole palm over hers. I left it there. Her eyes stopped moving. She looked right into my eyes, but she wasn't searching for anything. She was observing the whole shadow of my gaze. She was looking at the shades of colour in my irises. She was calm now; I could feel that in her hand. I could feel her warming in my grasp and she stopped trembling.

She stood up. For that day, for that first, slow afternoon, we'd come as far as possible down the road towards each other. The rest, in time.

She didn't say anything. I watched her form, tall and slender, wrapped in a long skirt and dark cape like a priest, I watched her rush away and disappear through the door without even nodding goodbye.

Now I know she's there. Even if she never comes back. Two weeks have passed and I keep on writing her letters but I don't send them. She'll come back to get them if she wants them. I'm convinced she knows I'm still writing.

I dream of her every night. I dream of putting my lips on her neck or wrapping my arms around her the way I used to embrace other women – with pleasure and indifference. But while I squeeze her she lifts her eyes and looks at me and says, Now you're different. In her abandon, I feel something more powerful than I ever felt with the others, something incomparable to a few moans and giggles.

She knows who I am. And that doesn't scare her.

But these are dreams. She hasn't come back, and today I'm much worse. I stare at my face in the bathroom mirror. I look like I'm covered with dust; I'm grainy and out of focus like a photocopy. Even so, I'm me. My mouth, my nose, the shape of my chin.

I'm sleeping when she comes back. I don't know how long she's been sitting there on the white stool watching me sleep. It's six in the afternoon and the room is dark. There's no one else here. The other beds are empty. One person was released and the others are out in the corridors with their relatives: it's visiting time.

You stopped writing.

I looked at her but didn't answer for a long time. She didn't look away; she stared right back into my eyes. And her eyes were like a photograph – so perfect and still.

I brought you a book because I noticed you didn't have any, she suddenly says.

I finished them all and my mother took them home. I still have a few in here, I tell her, pointing to the metal cabinet.

Who knows why I suddenly look at the window. The sky is grey-blue. Swollen.

I would like to keep on looking at her, to follow the curves of her face, memorise the way her mouth moves when she talks, but I can't control my eyes. To listen to her voice while looking out of the window; the grey sky is beautiful. Her voice has the same shades as the sky, the same vibrations; she's swollen and intricate too.

There is silence in the room. An azure light that is turning blue. I stay still, looking out of the window while she reads. It's been so long since someone's read to me. It's lovely. The faraway sound of someone's voice reading from a book – as if it didn't belong to the person it belongs to. The writing becomes a warm living body. But that only happens when someone reads for you and for you alone. Here, submerged in this deep azure light, my body laid out, relaxed, the beam of the lamp that she's turned on to the book warm on my cheek, I am perfectly happy. I'm as happy as a baby snug in bed listening to his father or mother reading to him from his favourite book. I don't think I'm even following the meaning of the words she's reading. What counts is the sound, the particular music that the words and her voice create. An unrepeatable harmony between different qualities of sound.

When she claps the book shut the intense silence comes back. I turn to her. A dark cloud crosses her tired eyes and her mouth is trembling.

Are you OK?

Me asking her that. It's funny how roles get reversed sometimes. I'd like to climb out of bed and tuck her into my place. I would like to nurse her body, her lovely hands rough with cold, close her eyes with the tips of my fingers, and talk to her in a low voice until she falls asleep. That's exactly how it should be. She should be laid out, not me. I'm a man; she's a girl. What stupid things I think; we're probably the same age.

How old are you?

The question seems to surprise her, her eyes glimmer ironically.

Thirty.

You're older than me.

I smile.

Right, but you could've guessed that.

Ferocious, but happy, with her innocent smile.

She gets up. There's a precise moment between two movements: between the smile and her hand lifting to adjust a button on her shirt collar. In that moment arrives desire. It's so strong it clutches the breath in my lungs. I reach out towards her thighs and she lets me. I slip my hand into her skirt, opening it as if it were a book. Her legs, in nylon, are the smoothest things I've touched since I've been in here. Smooth as a flat rock washed by the sea. Smooth as a newborn's cheek cleansed with the sweet tears of rainwater. I burrow and the heat rises. My hand reaches out along the endless expanse of those legs, as if I am crossing an immense and marvellous territory. Her eyes are open and on mine. She's not frightened. The book falls and makes a loud sudden sound. I pull my hand back with a start. A nurse puts her head into the room to see what's happened, but she retreats again immediately. I only glimpse her white cap.

Time has returned. Time comes into the room and makes everything go back to how it was.

Balanced.

Now I'm in a hurry. I try to get up but it makes my head spin. Everything has shattered behind my eyes; fragments of things flicker and race back and forth, crashing into each other.

She's the one doing this, slipping away quickly towards the door, closing it, turning to look at me, pulling a thin packet out from between the pages of the book that fell to the floor, and opening it with a flick of her fingers. It's still her, stretching out over me, pulling the sheets and pyjamas from my body. She kisses my mouth, begging me not to speak.

A layer of rubber separates life from death. Bitter latex rubbing against the walls of her body. I'd like to slide into her. But that's impossible.

We both know what it is.

She's the one who moves. I listen. I follow her body's thrusts as they speed up. I listen to the sound of her breath, the beating of her heart between her breasts where she's holding my head tightly. I listen to her naked knees brushing against the sheets. I listen to all the words sounding inside my head, words I'd like to say to her but can't, since she begged me to keep quiet. I listen to my fear too.

Fear that the border country in which we are in harmony will shrink and disappear and we will find ourselves on the same side, on my side. This idea makes me hard. A sudden spurt, a contraction of my abdominal muscles. She understands where I am too. She takes my head in her hands and laughs. Her laughter is beautiful. One hand slides down between our legs, into the damp crevice where our sexes are locked together. Cool fingers pull me from her body. The swollen ball of condom falls to the floor. She laughs again. Again, I feel the desire to be inside her. She lifts her knee and with a sudden thrust, she's let me in.

Balanced. That feeling again.

I would like to tear her from me and scream. At the same time I want it to last for ever. I close my eyes, I open them. She laughs. She pushes against me, keeping me still with her hands. The room is dark now.

We're equal. We're on the same side.

What does she say? Her words mix with her laughter and sound deep and nonsensical, as if deformed by dark echoes.

You didn't understand, did you?

I close my eyes, again balanced. On one side, darkness and fear; on the other, a still lake under the light of a sun I remember from when I was a child.

On the same side.

The room is still the same, even in the dark: four walls, six beds, two tall windows that look out over the car park.

We're in the middle. Quiet and still like a lake under the light of a winter sun.

Snapshots

For MP, whose hands make music.

I thought that she'd stopped. But no.

She's turned into a very good spy. She knows where to find in my expressions and movements the sudden transports, or moments of surrender. She's vigilant, always on the alert, ready, week after week, to capture images of me.

I haven't known about it for long. A month, perhaps. I was looking for an old wooden napkin holder shaped like a sparrow to give to my daughter Sara. At the very bottom of a drawer full of tablecloths, I found an enormous blue album. I opened it. On the first page there was an eight-by-ten picture of me at the piano taken from behind. Written below it in red marker:

Tommaso, April 1985. Height, 3½ feet. Weight, 88 pounds.

I leafed through page after page of them until I came to the last, before the empty pages:

Tommaso, April 1995. Height, 3¼ feet. Weight, 79 pounds.

There were a lot from the last two months. There must have been about a hundred snapshots. Glued in there, page after page.

In this ordinary photo album, with a blue cloth cover and pages thick with glue, are ten years of my life.

Me at the piano taken from behind. Me in the garden, sitting with our dog Jove and Sara, a few months old. Me in the bathtub reading a newspaper. Me at the kitchen table, sitting in the tall chair, a pen in my mouth and eyes fixed on the wall. Me in bed, sleeping – hundreds of pictures of the same subject. And then there's me, Sara and Giuliano, our youngest, sitting on the side of an inflatable pool that's about to tip over. So many more images. From days I don't remember any more. Other images have stayed with me, but they're out of focus, less shiny than the paper of these photographs.

She's always liked to take pictures. But I had asked her not to take them of me, please. She could take pictures of places and things, the children, every corner of the house, anything else.

It bothered me to sit and pose with the idea that there was someone, camera in hand, ready to capture me, betray me.

I had the impression she'd stopped. The camera, the lenses, all her apparatus had been packed quietly away in a bag hidden on the top of the wardrobe.

I didn't think anything more of it.

I'd never been interested in seeing the pictures people took of me – maybe just the occasional close-up. I didn't care to know exactly what my body was like. How it was mutating. I knew my hands were strong and that my legs could support me. All I needed was to be able to walk to the piano. All I needed were my hands to play, to touch her and the children. My hands to touch and give shape to the world.

Me, Tommaso.

As for the measurements, there were and there still are the doctors. The regular, ongoing visits that have structured my life. Naked hands, smooth like soap; or rough, gloved hands, stinking of latex and disinfectant: hands that rub, tap, take blood or other bodily fluids. I've become used to the constant invasion: the tickle, the feel of their hands on me, the cold metal. The way that one always gets used to things, so used to them that one doesn't notice them any more. My mind focused on other things: a particular passage on the keyboard; the lacquered blue of the May sky striped with white; Sara's lips forming around her first words with a fleeting grace impossible to reproduce.

Still, the sky on some May afternoons, like now, seems so dense that we could sink into it, like sinking into glue.

Maybe she stopped seeing my body long before the photos. Otherwise I don't know how she could have managed.

She liked my hands and my mouth. Even now that's all she sees. Her eyes run over me, overlooking everything except my eyes, hands, mouth.

Maybe she needs a way to preserve the truth. She needs to keep on knowing what I was, what I am, she needs to document a knowledge that she is no longer capable of collecting and organising merely with her senses.

She stopped trusting what she saw.

I don't even know if she looks back over the photographs once she's taken them. Maybe she's keeping them for afterwards. For the extreme but not inconceivable possibility that one fine day she'll find that she no longer remembers anything about me.

I was very much alone before I met her. And I was convinced that I would always be so; yet I was happy, because I had music, and music filled me to bursting. I was never frightened of my body, I was inside it and the music was outside it. Everything else changed continuously – bones, tendons, muscles that twisted and con-tracted – but inside, I remained the same. Everything, inside and out was constantly changing appearance, yet the centre stayed immovable. In bed at night I wrapped my fingers around smooth hot flesh, swollen with blood, and I could feel there was no difference between that and my heart: two pumps that emptied out and filled up again, two centres, two nuclei bound together and bound to me, never to abandon me. Like my hands, which never changed either. Though in contrast to the rest of me, they seemed to get bigger and stronger.

When I ran into people who hadn't seen me for a long time I'd see their eyes widen, see them get scared – they'd stay scared until they realised my hands were still intact.

The first time: she took me in her arms and conducted me to bed. It was a small, quiet hotel hidden in the midst of red and yellow hills, lit up by the June sun. Until then, we had only talked. We'd had no contact except for that moment at dinner when we both reached for the water pitcher at the same time and our bare arms brushed. It made a strange impression on me. Her arm was covered in slightly rough blond hairs like a sage leaf.

I could feel her body slowly leaning towards the centre of the bed, slowly until she was just touching me. Her right arm slid under my body and she pulled me over on to her. My toes grazed her thighs and my mouth only reached the nook of her neck. I looked up at her face and she was still, her lips parted and eyes closed. She wrapped me in her arms. I was in her.

It never changed after that. The gentle and decisive way that she'd taken me into her body the first time: no comments, requests, observations. It's still that way, simple, like releasing your muscles in deep water.

I've thought a lot over these years and I've thought many different things. Every time I hear her breathe, every time I see her muscles grow taut with pleasure, I've asked myself what exactly it is that she enjoys. Whether it's my hands, or my body, if it is me, all of me.

I never managed to understand how she could feel so much desire for me.

Then I thought that the ways are many, everyone is inclined to desire differently. She'd built her desires on me.

Before her, I'd always paid for women and I'd have to ignore their disgust, or fear. I had to avoid really touching them. I never allowed myself to caress their hair, touch their lips. I watched them undress, watched the hems of their dresses flutter to the floor, dust the ground. I watched them take off their lingerie, their movements both inviting and utterly personal: they weren't doing it for me; they were doing it for themselves, thinking about the money, about their next appointment, the shopping, walking the dog. Who knows what they were thinking of.

She laughed the first time. We woke early in the morning and the light was coming into the room at a slant and bouncing over the bed. The sheets had fallen to the floor. We were naked in all that white. She looked at me for a long time, her eyes swollen with sleep, and then suddenly her face widened and she began to laugh. She couldn't stop. Many men would have been offended, but I felt something special in her laughter, a happy, spontaneous sound, like the one babies make when something excites them.

She touched me – first with her hands, then with her lips. I could feel her hair falling between my legs and it made me laugh too. She pushed me down on to the bed and brought her mouth to my ear. Her laughter fell on me like rain. I don't know how long we stayed there, hugging and laughing. We had stomach cramps and couldn't catch our breath.

It was an odd moment. She came to me as if from far away, heading right for me, dodging thousands of people to get to me. She came with all their looks upon her – yet she was brand new. She brought many things with her: roads she'd travelled, the people and objects she'd touched, and she delivered it all to me. Everything that she'd seen, felt, touched was mine.

That dawn of laughter was a kind of ceremony for me, and I think it was for her too. The mutual exchange of all the suffering we'd passed through before we met. A suffering that melted all at once, in a long fit of laughter.

Ten years have passed.

And she's been spying on me for ten years. I can't believe it's happened. It was all so easy for me. And she let me believe it. She let me believe that it was easy for her too. Instead, she'd stopped trusting her eyes. Fear had attached itself to her thoughts and had altered them.

She's sleeping now. I watch her face, soft with sleep, travelling off to places I'll never be able to reach. A thread of saliva drops from her parted lips to her chin and then on to the pillow. It leaves a shiny trail. I'd like to pass my finger over it, dry it, but I'm scared I'll wake her. And I don't want to. I need to make a decision. I've been thinking about it for such a long time that I can't remember any more the specific reasons why I should or shouldn't. Right and wrong don't have strict boundaries, they mix, they cease to exist. There are only things you do or don't do, that change everything, or else change nothing. You don't know.

I look at her again.

Is this for me or for her? Am I the one who wants to forget, or do I want her to forget?

I believe that what I want is for her to see again, without having to impose it upon herself. I'd like her to open her eyes, now, and see me clearly.

Her muscles contract under the sheets. I see her legs tightening and then releasing, her eyelids trembling as if she is about to wake up, but then she turns suddenly and her hair wraps itself around her neck, a strand falling into her open mouth. She sleeps. Maybe she dreams.

I think I've learned things from other people. From healthy people, I mean. My relationship with things, however, with objects, measurements, proportions, is totally personal – it's something I couldn't share with anyone.

The height of a table, the knobs on a door, the shelves in a bookshop. Shop windows, counters in bars. Seats in a car, street signs, the gap between the train and the platform.

I've lived a strange life. I've seen everything from a different point of view; I interpreted the world's signals according to my own code. In the same way, other people have interpreted me differently and distantly from how I really am. They've felt fear, repulsion, pity and tenderness.

For a long time I felt like I was wearing a mask, as if there was something separating me from other people. Something that distinguished me, and made me constantly visible. But I couldn't take it off. I couldn't say, OK, guys, joke's over. That's enough looking. Don't be scared, it was just a joke. That's what I was, and I was me in the morning when I woke up, and I was me at night, during the day, on the street, at school. Me. A body that changed every day and wouldn't stop changing even when my adolescence was over. I would be like a teenager my whole life; someone who would have to live with muscles, bones and features that were constantly changing and altering his appearance.

Now that so much time has passed since I learned how to be myself, I think what I've felt and learned is priceless and that the way I play the piano doesn't come simply from my head, but from the particular structure of my body. From the constantly changing relationship of my hands to the rest of me. And what applies to the music, applies to her too. It explains the pleasure that, every day of our life together, I have seen suffuse her body and her eyes when she makes love to me. I am happy. What's more, I've made other people think, I've forced them to admit that there's more than one way, one knowledge and one single interpretation.

I've said it with music. And with my body.

I don't want her to force herself to remember, or to see in a scientific way something that she already sees in the right way. I don't want her to torture herself trying to see what others see, so that she can say, Oh yes, now I see the same thing.

I decide on her behalf. I decide while she's sleeping and doesn't realise what's happening.

I still don't know if it's right. I'll never know.

I take this big blue book – ten years of attentive looking – and I go downstairs. On the stairway, the cat slinks silently by me, its big soft paws moving in time with its undulating tail.

There is no precise way to look, my dear. It doesn't exist, it shouldn't exist. You shouldn't want it to exist. Restrain your eyes, the way I restrain mine. Measure the world without asking if you are seeing it in the same way as everyone else.

This is what I think. This is what I'd like to tell her.

The kitchen fireplace is still alight. Red embers glow under the ash. I blow on it, and wave a newspaper. I gather my strength. I add some kindling and a log. The blue album sits on my lap. I leaf through it. I'm always different. Sometimes the changes are imperceptible but there, hidden in some insignificant detail. The illness wears a mask, plays hide and seek, but never retreats. I turn the pages quickly, and revisit days and things, though none of these images stays with me. My memories are different: more rock-solid, made of emotions, feelings. This sick man, who gradually folds in on himself and dries out like an old sweatshirt as the pages turn, is and is not me. I know I am him, but I don't feel it. Only his hands resemble me. The rest is a cloud tossed by the wind. Something that has nothing to do with me.

I take out the photographs one by one and let them fall into the fire. Until I reach the end.

The album is no longer heavy. Its stiff cardboard cover of dark blue cloth holds only thumb-worn pages sticky with glue.

Flesh

Body – naked and lit.
Body – by moon and sun.
Body – silent and waiting.
Body – recalls no single gaze.

Giovanni Giudici, 'Body'

In order to be able to say this is a clear night, I think there should be more stars. The sky is very blue; it sparkles like the surface of a swimming pool lit by underwater lights. But there aren't many stars. It's a giant sheet of the paper we used to make the sky for the Nativity scene when I was little – but minus the stars. We'd cut the stars out of gold paper, and then glue them on to the big blue sheet, making sure not to drip glue everywhere. Now, they sell paper with the stars already on it, and it's not the same. Building a sky, inventing constellations – that's the stuff of dreams when you're a child.

I walk slowly over the wet gravel path. The rubber soles of my shoes slip now and then and I almost lose my balance. I listen to the crunching of the little stones, and sometimes I get scared – I think I can hear other feet crunching, as if someone is following me. But there's never anyone there. I know that perfectly well. There's never anyone there. If there were, well then, I certainly wouldn't be here.

I like the night. I like it because it's never the same. If you don't think about it too much, you might say that the night is dark.

That's a common thing to say. The night is dark; the sun is hot; it's wet when it rains.

Of course the night is dark, but it's never dark in the same way. Sometimes there's a full moon, other times it's waning: a little sliver, or no moon at all. Sometimes there's a spread of clouds superimposed on the moon, and those clouds might be grey, black, furrowed with white and blue, textured or silky, ruffled or straight. It depends.

It's never the same night and I'm always walking under a different sky, under a different sheet of blue.

It is the same with skin. You might say: what lovely white skin. Or else: alabaster, dark, golden, rosy, tanned, coffee- or honey-coloured.

They're all attempts to describe something impossible to describe. That's always different, elusive. Skin changes from one moment to the next, continuously morphing into something else – according to the temperature, or a person's emotions. Skin colours with anger, passion, fear; it shrivels and blushes in the cold wind; it burns and darkens under the sun; after a bath, after the gym; after making love it turns red and soft like a baby's skin, brushed with light. It can be white and blue like a Rubens. Generous flesh, with hints of pink and pale blue, and just a touch of green in the shadows.

As I walk down this gravel path, my bag slung over my shoulder, I think of such things. And I think how much I still have to learn about light and colour. You never have enough experience to make rules about the way things are.

But I'm running out of time.

I've got all my equipment with me in my bag.

I walk under the ever-changing night sky and listen to the rattling of objects in my bag. Lenses in their black plastic cases, the flash, rolls of film in their boxes, extra batteries, a collapsible tripod. A chamois cloth to polish the lenses. Objects I've carried with me for a long time.

I still remember the first photo I ever took. But I remember it in two distinct ways, for there were two shots, two images: there was the picture I took, and then there was the image engraved on my retina – what I saw just before taking aim and releasing the shutter.

In one image, the real picture, you see my mother sleeping. Her lips are parted, her facial muscles are relaxed, which makes her seem much older. Her hair is loose over her shoulders. Her lower teeth peek out in a crooked row between her lips. A soft light spreads over her forehead, giving her a kind of halo.

The other image, the one that only I have seen – that drove me to take that first picture, with the first roll of film threaded into my brand-new camera – is unforgiving. The light carves her face, digs out her cheeks, her skull is visible under her slackened skin.

I saw her the way she would be later. I saw her dead.

It was probably that first picture which formed my predilection for portraiture. I like to shoot people sleeping. I have photographed every woman I ever slept with, as well as friends, family, people in the waiting rooms at train stations, people dozing in their seats on the trains, their temples resting against the windows. People asleep on the grass in parks, sweaters rolled up under their heads.

But all these photos were different from the image I saw with my naked eye.

I never managed to reproduce that. I remember all the photos developed alone in the dark room which I had built in my country house. My heart pounded as I slid the paper from one pan of solution to the next, the pincers shaking between my fingers as I waited to see the image appear – at first just a shadow, then growing clearer. Or, if I used a lab in the city, I'd go to pick them up, I'd pay and put away the receipt, I'd get into my car and open the envelope right away, sitting there in the parked car.

But they were never like the image I had seen. That image remained somewhere else, lost inside me like a splinter of glass. The photos in front of me were different. They were of sleeping people: a dear and familiar face, or the ghost of a stranger I'd met in the city during my endless wandering. Faces asleep, muscles slack, eyes closed, lashes quivering, strange shadows crossing the cheeks and forehead, the harsh shadows of some unknown dream. You could tell the people were alive, that they were only sleeping. The images I had first seen had been different. I had glimpsed a secret and frightening place. I had seen those faces as they would look afterwards. I'd seen a skeleton emerge through the soft skin, clear and stiff like an iron mask. The shape wasn't like anything else. It was pure. Although it has no effect to say it like that.

I was thirty years old the first time I took a night-time walk. I think it might even have been my birthday. It was March, the night was clear and cold, like tonight. I hadn't planned anything in particular. Everything I'd been thinking for so many years, through school, and then college, while I studied physiology – a subject I soon abandoned – everything became condensed. It all came to a cool, distinct head. It all came true. I stopped making up theories. I stopped imagining things. What I wanted to see was close at hand. It was right there, like everything that you desperately want and that seems so impossible. It's not. In reality, it's all right there. What's frightening is the act of taking it. What you want to know, what you're obsessed by – it's the only real motive that drives you through life, that gets you out of bed every morning. And once you reach it, you know there's nothing more in front of you. A flat and deserted horizon. The void.

But I wasn't frightened that night. I was walking through the dark cold of my little town on the plains. I heard the crunch of bicycle wheels as some old man rode home from his card games and drinks at the bar on the piazza. Pebbles shot out from under the tyres. An owl cried softly between the branches of the plane trees. I walked. I put one foot in front of the other without thinking of anything except the way my calf muscles tightened and loosened, the way my toe joints popped in the warm comfort of my worn leather shoes.

I could see the shadow of the church in the distance, a massive silhouette with soft arabesque curves. There was an iron fence, and a row of tiny lights quivering in the night. The silence was thick, layered with sounds so faint you can hear them only if you've lived on the plains for long enough, if you've lived away from the city and its strident noise – noise that gets in your head and never leaves.

They'd buried her that afternoon. I didn't know her, though I'd heard about her. I don't think our paths had ever crossed. She was off studying at the university in Bologna. She was twenty-five years old. She had a stroke one night while she was in her room reading. She went like that, one cold flash. Senseless. Her eyes were still fixed on her open book. Her hands still resting on the table. She'd been reading Dante for her thesis on Italian literature, copying down quotations, writing out the bibliography, organising index cards in a small metal box.

I chose her because of how perfect her death had been. There'd been no accident to distort her face or body, no sickness to consume her features: it had been quick and painless and the expression on her face never changed.

She was like someone asleep, yet she was more. She was there in the dark place that I'd only glimpsed – like an out-of-focus slide projection in my head.

It wasn't difficult to pull her coffin from its compartment in the vault. It was conveniently placed on the bottom row. A strange place to be, as the dead are usually put in ascending order – with the more recent ones at the top. But, I think they start again from the bottom when they exhume the older corpses, the ones that have already turned to dust.

I wonder who they took out in order to make space for her, for her new body. There must be some kind of meeting when the places are changed. A silent salute.

I pulled the coffin towards me in a cold embrace, slowly lowering the bottom edge to the ground and carefully sliding it forward. I ran my hands over the smooth surface of the lovely pale wood. I caressed it, as if she would be able to feel from within that I only wanted to touch her gently, to look at her the way no one would ever look at her again. Mine would be the last look, the real look. Because true things are those which are definitive, and things are only definitive for a short time. Like her. She was only just dead, definitively dead, yet she would change soon, she would become something else. Her body would move through one stage after another, until it disappeared entirely. She was in the last remaining moments of that human form we call the body.

I didn't have any idea what to expect. I wasn't frightened, but I preferred to wait. Everything had to be perfect: my movements, my eyes. I couldn't be trembling, or distracted by thoughts that took me elsewhere. I was there to look at her, and to deliver that look to eternity. It was better to wait, to wait some more, to wait until I felt that all thoughts had abandoned me, that even the most imperceptible resistance had disappeared. To wait until I was ready.

I smoked a cigarette. My gaze wandered over the tops of the cypress trees that encircled the garden and marked its perimeter. It was a beautiful night. I felt so peaceful, so close to a possible resolution. The days and nights had been passing heavily over me for so long – or had been empty and motionless. I was light. We were both light – me and the night.

I took out the screws and put them into my right trouser pocket. I gently pulled off the lid and laid it on the ground. I inhaled deeply the sweet perfume of her body mixed with the night air.

Wet grass, earth and flesh.

I kneeled before her, my eyes still closed. I waited for the darkness to enter my mind. Then, finally, I looked.

She wore a white dress, like a maiden from the eighteenth century. Her ash-blond hair, though, was cut short. I focused on her dress and her hair for a long time. The perfume of her body was sweet, too sweet. But it didn't bother me. That smell has never bothered me. We are. We are also that smell. When you've smelled it once, you never forget it.

On the middle finger of her right hand, she wore a silver ring with a purple stone. It was a cheap piece of jewellery, a little girl's ring.

But I wasn't interested in those things. I didn't want to know anything about her.

It was her face I wanted to see.

I brushed a strand of blond hair from her forehead, still without looking at her face. I made myself concentrate on the palpable stiffness of her hair which must have been so soft once.

Her cheeks were hard and white, smooth like marble. Her flesh had gone cold. It stuck to her bones. A perfection that couldn't possibly have been there when she was alive, laughing or chewing, muscles moving to distort the lines.

But I couldn't describe her in words.

I photographed her.

I turned on the flash and waited until the orange light came on.

I clicked immediately: once, twice, three times, holding my breath. Then I inhaled, and shifted angle. I took another.

I lingered on her face: her nose, her lips slightly parted, eye-lashes over shut eyes – two white spheres that held the secret of their colour. I needed to see. I pulled her eyelid up, feeling the slightest give under the tip of my index finger. But I couldn't tell what colour her eyes were in that light. I saw all colours: blue, grey, white, black.

It's one thing I can't say for sure. I'm unable to report on the colour of her eyes. Living eyes and dead eyes are very different.

I lowered her eyelid, pushing slightly so she wouldn't remain with one eye open and one closed, as if she were winking at someone, without malice and without a smile.

I loosened the top buttons of her dress and freed her neck. She had a long delicate neck, a Parmigianino without all the golden flesh tones. Her skin colour was a lot closer to one of those poor bodies in a Bill Henson image. Moon white, with long, barely perceptible brush strokes of blue and purple.

I touched her skin. Cool and hard. I undid another button, then another. Her breasts appeared. Pale and firm like snow sculptures.

I took a lot of pictures, from every possible angle.

I lifted her long white dress and her two little bare feet appeared, then her slender calves, already a bit swollen. Her fingernails were round and painted opalescent white.

I photographed everything: her feet, her calves, her nails.

Then I rested. I lit a cigarette and tried to recapture that feeling of serenity and neutrality. But thoughts were bombarding me. I squashed them, and then more came. They kept coming back, sharp and cruel.

The word *necrophiliac* came into my mind. Is that what I was then?

A man all alone undressing a dead woman to take pictures of her naked. What is it, if it isn't necrophilia?

But not me. I kept repeating that to myself. It looks like that, but it isn't.

Yet my hand flicked away the cigarette butt and slid back down into the coffin. My hand gathered the hem of her dress and lifted it higher. Her thighs were pale and unmarked. She had the legs of a statue. And further up, where her thighs joined at her sex, there was nothing but a triangle of white fabric, soft and thin, that must have been silk.

Things came into my mind again that I didn't want to think. Who chose what underwear she was going to wear in her coffin? Her mother, a little sister? It couldn't have been a man. Certainly not. A man would have been ashamed to be thinking about these sorts of thing for a dead girl. He would have been horrified. Women are different. They aren't frightened of the body. They don't worry about obscenity. That tiny scrap of white silk must have been a tribute from a sister or her mother – someone who'd loved and respected the girl's beauty. Maybe she always wore things like that and wouldn't have wanted plain, modest underwear. It was a final gesture of love, though not without the bold flirtation that women share among themselves.

I lifted the camera and shot more, then more.

I let my eyes slide over her one last time. That poor body I would be the last to see. I pulled down her dress and refastened the top buttons. I smoothed the pleats with the palm of my hand, trying to give it the same freshness and poise it had before.

If this is the end of all things, this calm sleep that dissolves in silence, then it's not that horrible. It's the same thing that happens to the leaves every autumn. It's the same for all living creatures: a calm sleep that slowly dissolves.

I put the screws back and tightened each one carefully. There was a beautiful silence around me. The lights of the little cemetery seemed like party lights set up in the middle of a field.

It was harder to put her back than it had been to slide her out, but I forced myself not to rush in case I dropped her. Afterwards, I put the stone back in its place and I packed my camera and equipment back into the bag.

I headed home and felt the dawn arrive. A gentle tremble and just a hint of light blue in the dark.

Back home I got into bed and fell fast asleep. My hands still smelled of her.

She was the first and there were others after her. But I'd rather not talk about them, except to say that I always selected them in the same way. The way I'd chosen her on that distant night.

Not one of them was as significant, and not one of them was as beautiful. But they all shared a dignity and strength that living people don't have – except in rare moments. They were there. They couldn't stand up and say something stupid. They couldn't hurt someone or be ridiculous. They were dead, and that conferred on to them an ineffable aura. They were all God.

I print the pictures myself. I keep them in notebooks made out of recycled paper, each picture covered with a thin sheet of protective film. I don't put names or dates. I never look at them again. I haven't looked at them once. I keep them for someone else, for someone like me, who will need to see.

I've been peaceful for so long. It isn't important what's happened in my life, or what I've done, who I've lost along the way, or who I never took along with me. Mine has been a life like many. Sometimes happy, and other times more complicated and troubled. But one thing has never diminished, and that is the certainty I felt that first night, that a sweet calm, just like sleep, waits for all things that move on this earth. Men, animals, plants. A tranquil, dreamless sleep. Unmovable like all the things we know can never be.

It's March again. I walk down the gravel path, my bag on my back, now as worn out and faded as I am.

I don't take pictures any more. I just bring the camera out of habit, to feel its familiar weight against my hip. I've come out here to walk, think, relax and smoke a cigarette in the company of all my silent friends. It won't be long before I join them. And I'm not frightened. I'll end up here too, in this festive garden in the fields. I'll have a stone, and a rectangular space. I'll rest quietly while time does what it must. I'm not frightened. Is laying down to sleep at night frightening? First, there are tempests, battles, tears, frustration, and sudden bursts of joy. Then a calm, silent sleep that slowly dissolves. That's all.

The Woman on the Cliffs

The Body – borrows a Revolver –
He bolts the Door –
O'erlooking a superior spectre –
Or More –

Emily Dickinson, 'Composition, number 670'

I read in an old newspaper that a woman threw herself off the cliffs last summer. It was the middle of the day. The sun was reflecting peacefully off the sea, and the children were running on the beach with their buckets and spades raised high like bayonets.

What sound did her body make when it struck the rocks below?

No one on the beach heard. Because of the waves and the wind. They saw her fly down, out of nowhere, while with wet and greasy hands they applied their sunscreen.

A fleeting white form, first elongated then suddenly crumpled like a piece of paper covered in mistakes. Her hair streaming upwards. A dark yellow cone. Feather-light and pointed.

But I'm inventing all these details. The newspaper just reported the facts. Succinct and to the point.

I see everything. I imagine her.

Maybe because I stood on that same cliff one day. I, too, thought that if I ever wanted to kill myself, I would do it there. Some places attract suicide. I don't know why. It's just that way. Everyone thinks about it when they see cliffs. Some people try it. Some succeed. I have never understood what it depends on. It's not just a question of height. Or vertigo. Maybe it's how the light falls during a certain hour of the day, how much of and what part of the sky you can see. The smell of the air. The unexpected desire to let that place hold you like a hand. The last hand.

I don't have very much to do today. Nothing for work, no one to meet, no telephone calls to make or wait for.

I fold the newspaper back up. After that article, I don't want to read anything else.

I'll cook something, then I'll invite someone to dinner.

I let the day pass. I look out of the windows. I talk to myself, or to the dog.

This house is still new to me. I'm not used to the lighting, where the walls are, how many steps it takes to cross each room. I look around the kitchen. It's the only room in the house where I feel safe.

That's probably because cooking is my favourite pastime. I like to invent recipes, play with spices like a painter mixing colours, one drop at a time. I like to transform things, watch ingredients turn into something else in my hands.

But I also like to copy recipes. That's why every time I go somewhere new I buy a cookbook of the local cuisine, or I find one of those typical restaurants – the kind where there's still an old lady who knows everything and will tell you all her secrets. I copy the best recipes into a big binder which is subdivided into courses: appetisers, pastas, meats, sauces, side dishes, desserts. I like to leaf through my binder, even when I'm not planning to cook anything. There's different coloured paper for each section, thin paper that smells like vanilla because I keep a little stick of vanilla in there. I remember a lot from when I was little and would watch my grandmother prepare batter for *torta paradiso* or *sfogliatelle*. The kitchen was full of sun, all orange and dark pink, and grandma's hands moved quickly and surely. Every now and then she'd look up at me and smile. I think that's my most beautiful childhood memory.

The kitchen is the prettiest room in the house, and the only one I'm really devoted to. I planned it and built it with my own two hands. I spent whole nights selecting materials and designing the shape for the worktop. A kitchen is not a real kitchen unless it has a worktop, a large empty surface where you can line up all the ingredients, work with them and transform them into masterpieces. A surface that doesn't make you choose to do one thing before another, a surface that accommodates everything you're going to need.

All along one wall, I installed chrome rods with lots of little hooks to hang my utensils. They are lovely, shiny and cold, like a mechanic's tools. They are all different shapes and sizes: knives, garlic presses, parsley choppers, tongs.

I think of my mother's kitchen in the old house where we used to live. I can see the greasy tiles, the work surface covered with junk. Encrusted pots with loose handles. My mother didn't like cooking, and still doesn't like it although she's old and doesn't have anything else to do. Instead of making food, she prefers gardening: pulling weeds, planting bulbs, her knees buried deep in the damp soil, her fingers stuck full of thorns.

She's always been thin. I think that's why she never liked to cook, so she could stay thin.

This kitchen is different from the one where I spent my childhood. Different from the kitchen where my mother taught me to fear butter, animal fat, sausages, sweets. All the stuff that goes in your mouth and ends up on your hips. That's what she said every time she put food to her lips.

My kitchen is a peaceful kitchen, the workshop of a happy alchemist. An alchemist who isn't worried about hidden cholesterol and the calorie count of each mouthful. Food is my link to the world, it's my love, it nourishes my life and fills it.

I keep thinking about the woman. But along with the sad image of that tiny form falling as if it were made of nothing, something else, a peculiar joy is rising in me. It happens whenever I cook. It's like a celebration. I begin preparations in the afternoon and I can already imagine my guests' faces when they see the duck à l'orange – glossy and fragrant, stretched out on the silver platter – or the vegetable terrine – the aspic shimmeringly ethereal and clear as an aquarium, hugging the green broccoli, delicate slices of tomato, chopped carrots and tender peas. I love to watch their lips stretch over forkfuls of meat stuffed with onion, or little croquettes of spinach and ricotta. The murmur of pleasure as the delicacies burst on their palate. Watch their throat muscles contract as it all slides down into the safe hot shelter of the stomach.

I can't stop thinking about it. As I knead the dough I go over the details.

Maybe I'd seen her. Walking around the village. Maybe I brushed her elbow. In the supermarket. Maybe when I was swimming in the bay in front of the village, maybe our paths crossed then. I can't remember. They didn't print her name in the paper. Just her initials: G. M. And her age: thirty-four. Four years older than me.

I keep thinking of the children playing on the beach. If they saw her, and what they saw. What did they think they were seeing? What did they say afterwards?

I call Giada. She's free tonight. I tell her to bring whoever she wants – Giovanni, Piero, whoever's around. I can fit up to ten people at my table. While we're making up the list, I almost tell her about the old newspaper and what I read. But I keep quiet. I don't know why. I'm scared. It's as if the story of the woman on the cliffs might reveal a secret about me. As if by telling her I would suddenly be naked in front of her.

And I don't want to be. Or, maybe I do, even if it scares me. When I hang up, there's an unbearable tightness in my stomach.

My heart's pounding and all the words I might have said to Giada are sitting there in my stomach, speeding around, in fits and starts as if they were alive.

I put my hand over it.

It's taut, like a drum. The skin is tight and feels like it's about to burst. I can feel protuberances with my fingertips, hard as stones, little monsters running around inside me. Alien bodies, infesting and destroying. My fingers run up and down the hostile perimeter, trying to keep the monsters back, to block them. But they know that I can't.

It won't take much. The bathroom is so close. The door is open. I bow my head over the bowl, I kneel. Here I am, in position.

It's like a prayer.

This: every day.

My hand is weak as it crosses my lips. My fingers slide over my rough tongue, over my teeth, until they find the right position, a dark, scarred hole into which they fit perfectly.

Here I am.

The first heave is always the hardest. But it comes. A flurry of aliens sliding out and screaming, climbing up my throat, gripping the walls of my oesophagus with tentacles of fire.

The sound is of lots of tiny bodies diving into water.

I wipe my mouth with my hand. The stink of gastric juices mixed with food no longer troubles me.

What I do afterwards is for others.

But I'm still not done. I know there are still more in there. The rebels, the ones I have to force out. I put my head under the tap and drink. The water soothes the wounds, cools the burning. The water fills me up, fills me up and doesn't do any harm. And then it comes back out again. It cleans me, rips all the stubborn, clinging things from the depths of my stomach.

I clean my mouth and face with toilet paper, and throw it into the bowl. I flush again. I rub my forehead and run my hands through my sweaty hair. I wash my face and gargle with cool mint mouthwash.

I do all this and try to avoid the reflection of my face in the mirror.

A prayer.
This: every day.

Now those words I wanted to say and didn't say aren't there any more. They left me. Slipped away down the toilet. But I still see her. I distract myself by soaking the sheets of gelatin in water. I slice the carrots, cut thick blocks of ham. I get my hands dirty. When I smell them, the odours have become so mixed up they don't smell like anything any more.

I fill the dog's bowl to overflowing with meat. A few mouthfuls fall to the ground. He'll clean them up with his flat, sandpapery tongue. He'll lick away the grease spot on the tiles too. He's a good boy.

I sit on the ground and watch him dunk his furry snout into the bowl. His whiskers tremble happily, his plump little tail waves in the still air of the room. I listen to his jaw move, the breathless chewing, the saliva gurgling in his gullet.

Her house might be right near mine. Maybe her eyes looked up at my windows many times and I never saw or felt anything.

As if it were my fault. As if I could have saved her.

But I have to stop thinking about it.

Compelling: the expressions of dogs when they want you to do something for them. He looks up at me. He looks at his lead hanging on the wall.

I know you want to go out.

I'll get up now. I'll take him out now. But he needs to clean the bowl first. I want to see him burst. I want his stomach to get hard and round, an enormous watermelon. I want to watch the fat accumulate on his back and hips. It's nice to be fat. To carry around all that love for the food you've swallowed, all the tenderness of a lover or friend who has held to your lips a hunk of bread stained with sauce, an oyster quivering in lemon juice, a block of dark chocolate. It's wonderful to fill oneself up, to bathe in the sweet fullness of the flesh, the density of the substances that, minute by minute, are becoming a part of you. To be whole. To occupy space. To feel your own body under your fingers, existing, growing. It must be wonderful.

For other people.
   Not for me.
   I disappear. And I'm reborn. Delicate like a wedding veil; slender like a blade of grass.

We just need to turn the corner at the end of the street and we're in open country. The peaceful fields are beautiful here. The air is cool and the grass is waving, full of its little secrets. I untie him and watch from afar as he leaps and lunges out into the middle of the grass, his tongue hanging out.

In the meantime, I watch the stars. And I keep thinking about it. Sunk in my thoughts I try to understand why I'm clinging to the image of her flying off the cliffs.
   I see her from behind, a slight figure, still looking down, standing still – even though she's already made up her mind.
   She seems like a child. She's wearing a pale yellow and white dress, with little flowers. It's a summer dress that lifts in the breeze to reveal straight, thin legs, little girl legs. She looks like she's only seven years old, ten at most. For some reason though, I've decided she's seven.

Why should a seven-year-old girl want to die?

The sky has turned black. It happens quickly, in December. It's already so dark it seems like night and I still haven't finished preparing dinner. My guests are arriving in less than two hours. I must run home. Whistle, and the dog is in front of me.

But I'm so tired now I need to lie down. Five minutes. Just five.

The dog sleeps at the other end of the bed. I reach a foot down, to stroke him with the tip of my toe. His fur is short and rough.

I can't sleep. I keep thinking about that woman.

I close my eyes in the dark and the black becomes more black.

I dream about the woman on the cliff. She's sitting in front of a giant birthday cake. White and pink icing, decorated with hundreds of little red sweets in the shape of an erupting volcano. What a strange way of decorating a birthday cake, pink icing and a volcano. She blows on the candles. Her blond hair is a cloud around her ageless face; the cloud of hair moves as if it were alive. The flames won't go out under her powerful breath; they get bigger and sparkle gleefully.

I only have an hour to get everything done. There's no time for a shower, but that's not important. No one's going to notice that my hair isn't shampoo-fresh. Especially not Giada. She's always in a mess and in a hurry. I'll just wear some old sweater.

The terrine is perfect. Transparent as air. The forms are suspended in the limpid gelatin. Even the pasta sauce seems to have come out well. And all the rest.

I keep thinking about that dream as I spread the tablecloth.

My seventh birthday cake was decorated with red sweets.

Every Sunday when I was little, my father would take me to our beach house. We went alone because my mother had to stay at home with my little sister. My father drove fast and the flowers were beautiful along the side of the road. Fields of coloured flowers. I liked watching them fly by through the glass, seeing them mutate into a glowing stain of coloured confusion. I'd even squint a little to make them go even more out of focus. After a while, my head was spinning as if I'd drunk wine and it made me laugh. My father didn't like it when I laughed, I don't know why. It made him nervous. And so he accelerated, that afternoon of the year in which I turned seven.

And the flowers became nothing through my squinting eyes because of the speed.

But I still kept my eyes half shut and my head turned towards the fields, and that's why I didn't see the little girl running across the road, or our car running over her.

I like my new green crystal glasses. Giada will like them too, I'm sure of that. She likes things to be a little weird and she loves bright colours. The white wine takes on an acid glow, the colour of bitter tomatoes. The bouquet is grapefruit, apples and grass. I know I shouldn't start drinking when I'm alone. I know.

I really didn't see anything. My father grabbed my arm and covered my eyes. I stayed quietly in his arms although really I wanted to run away to the fields, because I hated him, and I still hate him, after all this time. My father smelled like a wild man.

He was disgusting.

That smell stayed on my skin afterwards.

The blackberry pie didn't help to make it go away. I had to force it down, with him watching me. But I couldn't keep it down. As soon as he looked away, I spat it out into my hand. The smell of blackberries mixed with the smell of my father made my stomach turn.

It didn't go away even after I'd scraped at my skin with the Horrible Sponge. That's what my sister called it. The Horrible Sponge was cold and hard, so abrasive it took off a layer of your skin. It was what my mother always used on us. She said that we were dirty, dirtier than anything. Dirty like gypsy babies. Dirty like someone had thrown us out with the rubbish.

I didn't see anything. After a while they put me in another car and took me to the local café where a lady gave me an orange squash which I drank. Then I fled the café and ran away down the narrow streets. I ran for a long time and thought my lungs were going to burst. When I got to the cliffs, I stopped suddenly and looked down. The waves were long and calm, the green of emeralds, the crests bursting with captured light. Jewels of green water. The orange squash came back up in my throat and I vomited. It fell slowly, weightless like foam, mixing into the seawater. I got a stain on the front of my yellow-flowered dress. I thought they were going to yell at me. But my father didn't say anything when he came back to get me. I got into the car and we went home.

My father never took me to the beach again after that day when I was seven. He didn't hold me in his arms any more. But I still have his smell on me just the same. It's never gone away. Out of everything, it's never gone away.

Maybe the woman who threw herself off the cliffs had the same kind of smell on her too.

Everyone is arriving now. My green crystal goblets twinkle in the candlelight. Giada is definitely going to like them.

I think of the cliffs at the edge of the village. This time of year, at night, they're immersed in deep blue. The water is smooth, still. It creeps over the stones, the sharp rocks. There's no foam. The sky, reflected in that black sheet of water, shines without a quiver. No one is there at this hour. The silence down there must be taut like a rope. Hard and cold, barely warmed by the chilly sweep of the lighthouse beam, opening and closing like an eye.

Things

There are perhaps things
with which
I didn't believe
until today
I would ever come into contact.

Kawasaki Hiroshi, 'Sea'

All that's left are his things. What his hands touched, moved, cleaned, wiped, washed, dried. What he caressed and held.

The dishes. The chipped blue plate. The tall brown mug also chipped – along the rim, where his lips used to rest. The yellow towelling basket full of perfume samples. The razor left on the edge of the sink in the bathroom, crusted with dry foam and little hairs. The black pencil he used to underline passages in the last book I saw him read, McEwan's *First Love, Last Rites*. The soft, blue cotton T-shirt with orange lettering ('Thank God I'm an atheist – Luis Buñuel') that he left hanging on the hook behind the kitchen door. The ball he modelled painstakingly out of aluminium foil one day he was bored at school many years ago. An ivory-coloured guitar pick lodged in the cushions of the armchair. A yellow silk rose on a bookshelf. A little silver angel perched on the end of a pencil. A carbon-fibre tennis racquet, very lightweight, with a pale purple cover and phosphorescent green tape on the handle.

Objects.
  Things.

My body has become a thing too. It has no more openings. It is closed. I don't know how it happened. I have the impression that all my seams are sealed shut. My vagina is as smooth and compact as a Barbie doll's. My mouth is welded shut. Even my toes and fingers seem different, attached somehow like a frog. My skin is the only thing that's alive, the only thing that reacts. And it only reacts upon contact with things. Smooth, cool surfaces or rough, warm ones. Damp, dry, hot, cool surfaces, surfaces that change temperature when I touch them. Touch has become sex for me.

Things are just like me. There have been a number of times when I've surprised myself by looking at objects with emotion. I see them left somewhere, abandoned, forgotten, incapable of moving. Alone. Each one different from the next, each one belonging to its own category, with its own particular physical make-up. Subject only to our will – we, the humans, who possess them, use them, forget them.

It's stupid even to have to say something so obvious: they are made up of atoms, the same stuff we're made of. They're existent, they have qualities, characteristics. They have names. But they're generic names that don't represent anything except what category each object belongs to. The names bear no emotional significance. I'd like to gather all the abandoned objects in the world into my house – especially the ones that have never been used, the newborns, the ones that have never lived in a real house or belonged to someone – and give each one a different name. I'd like to find them a place, the exact perfect place they would have chosen for themselves, if they were capable of choosing.

And then I'd like to hold them all close to me, feel them on my naked skin, one object at a time. To be able to close my eyes and recognise any kind of material by touch, by the way it feels on the surface of my skin.

That's the way it started – with his things after he left. The how and why of his leaving are unimportant. The how and why someone leaves someone else are always the same. Motive isn't important. One person stays and the other person goes. The one who's left takes everything that's his, usually – and usually, he forgets something. As aforementioned.

I slept with his blue T-shirt. I drank my morning coffee from the brown mug. I shaved my armpits with the crusty razor. I used the black pencil to write out my shopping list. I fiddled with the little ball of aluminium foil and the silk rose while I was organising my notes for work, or while I was talking on the phone.

My fingers touched the cotton, ceramic, plastic, wood, aluminium, and silk. I learned to recognise them. I'd shut my eyes and let my fingertips go searching for the skin that lay beneath the materials. But the bastards kept on being objects. I continued to touch them, every day. And my fingers got more and more sensitive to their feel. Little by little I realised that there was pleasure in it. A pleasure that was an end in itself, that grew day after day. It became sensual, so intense and total I thought I'd lose my mind.

I started going into shops in order to touch things.

I asked the assistants, the more pleasant ones who seemed trustworthy, to show me some object. I'd caress it from afar with my eyes. I'd anticipate the moment when my fingers would take possession of its substance. Then, I'd spot another object and ask the girl to show it to me, and then another, and then another. Initially, I'd ask a lot of questions: about the object's durability, when it was made, what it was made of, etc. Then, I learned to keep quiet, to find the answers by myself through my fingertips. The questions might have been my way of dispelling the fear and embarrassment, of taking my time.

Now I am furtive and skilled. I touch everything – in supermarkets too. Curtains, tablecloths, cans, utensils. Everything. I go into shops for the sole purpose of touching, department stores and hardware stores – especially hardware stores, a paradise of metal and plastic, tubes and insulation. The hardware store is my idea of sin.

I've worked for the Cultural Institute at 5 Via Farini for the last few years.

I work on a computer. My fingers tap at a keyboard six hours a day. My computer keyboard is soft and gummy; the keys barely depress under my fingers. The sound they make is muffled and sensual, regular, except for the space bar which has an unexpectedly metallic spring. The only variation in the rhythm of my working day is when I turn ninety degrees to the left on my rotating blue chair, and use the electric typewriter instead. It has a sharp, hard, unpleasant tap, but fortunately I don't have to use it that often.

There's a blind boy down at the reception desk. We've never said anything to each other except for Good morning, and Good night. But lately, there is so much that I want to ask him. I'd like to know, for example, if his fingers appreciate the difference between a polyvinyl coating and a rubber one on canvas. If he can tell the colour of things by how they feel. Whether the raised letters on a plastic container evoke for him the sweeping sound of leaves on a birch tree. If he agrees that Panini notebooks have the best laminated paper as far as texture goes. And whether he agrees that Simmenthal boxes – with their white porcelain insides – are superior to all other tin boxes, inside and out.

That sort of thing.

To get to Via Farini every morning, I walk down a long street. There's a kitchenware shop on the left at the intersection with Via Santo Stefano, where I waste at least a quarter of an hour every lunch break. I'm happy even just standing in front of the window, imagining the secret possibility of a Rowenta steam iron, with regulating functions and an extra-wide base, or the thickness of a raffia place mat, or a roll of Cuki baking parchment – which is the most resilient brand.

I only recently discovered POW. Somebody must have told me about it, I don't remember who. I do know that I got there the first time by following directions scrawled on a paper napkin from a restaurant.

POW. Plastic Objects Warehouse.

POW is in the town of Villanova di Castenaso, which is a few miles outside of Bologna in an industrial zone, just after a bend in the road. I hear it's been there for a long time, twenty years, maybe longer. It was formerly on the other side of the road, a little closer to the town centre, but then it got so successful they had to enlarge it and they bought a bigger warehouse. There are blue and yellow flags out on the road inviting you in.

I know people who spent their childhood at POW. It's the kind of place where everyone goes sooner or later. Who has never needed gardening tools, do-it-yourself kits, cups, plates, stools, card tables, tubing, plastic shower curtains, or rubber mats?

It's always crowded, especially on Saturday. There's a car park at the front, and as soon as you park and have a chance to look around, you realise that the people who go there are possessed, electrified. It's even worse than in a supermarket. I don't know why this kind of place is so stimulating. I don't believe that all those people are driven by the same impulses as I am. But I can see a certain perversion in all of them. It's not just the desire to acquire, there's something of a fetish there. They tap the rubber tubing to test its thickness. They move from one aisle to the next with an expert air. They hand-weigh clothes pegs as if they were precious gems. They open and close drying racks to test their stability. They compare the capacity of various vases, tubs, buckets, food storage containers and dog-food dishes. They finger the vinyl upholstery. When they leave, with shopping trolleys stuffed to the brim, their eyes are dull and empty. Sated.

When I come home from the office, my first concern is the house. The objects. I dust them and reposition them. I look at them. I walk naked around the house, marvelling at the incredible quantity of stuff I've accumulated.

It's all new. When it comes to objects, I can't stand the idea that they've been used by someone else, that they carry a story, that they've already been in a house, in someone's hands, or that they've represented something in someone else's life, that they've played a role in someone else's intrigue.

In the beginning, it was about his things, what was left behind. In the beginning I'd look to his objects to find human warmth. Now that I've come to know these things, I love them for themselves. I like things to be neutral, without a history, free from the inevitable beating that life delivers. I want them in their packages, dusty from having sat on a shelf in a shop for too long. I even like the wrappings. I like the plastic packages the best, the bubble wrap they use around fragile objects. Those bubbles drive me wild. I bite them, trying to make them pop. I suck them. I roll them in my mouth, trying to squash them with my tongue, or suck them flat until they burst on my gums.

I watch TV too when I'm home. I eat convenience food – pizza, or a Chinese takeaway. I spread the food out on my sea-green plastic tray with the extendable legs. I sit on the ground, on my new carpeting that I haven't glued down yet, or even unrolled the whole way. The carpet is ice-coloured, made of this indestructible material. I'd say it's clingy. That's the impression it gives me when I lie down naked and feel it under my back and legs, or tummy. Clingy, with just a little of the roughness of natural fibres, but cooler, almost elastic.

Most of the TV shows are boring. The only thing that really sparks my interest is the shopping channel. Between slices of pizza and mouthfuls of mineral water – either Levissima, which has a pink label, or Rocchetta, which has a blue label – I note down in my diary telephone numbers, prices, sizes, special features.

There was an advertisement for a stomach flattener: black, tight, invisible so you can wear it under your clothes. In the ad there's a girl teetering around on high heels, wearing only a bra and this girdle, as if it were a dress. Every two or three seconds, she pauses and rolls the girdle down with her thumbs to show you the pearly beads of sweat on her abdomen. The girdle is shiny and thin, so thin that you can almost see her skin's imperfections through it. I want to call that company and find out if they can make me a whole bodysuit out of that material. It would be beautiful to be able to wear something like that all day long under my clothes. Much better than those other weight-loss bodysuits made out of stiff, crackling plastic that rubs and irritates your skin.

Last night I fell asleep on a patch of synthetic grass that I bought at POW yesterday afternoon. The grass was so inviting, so green. It looked damp with dew, emerald green, mint green, thirst-quenching cool. I asked them to cut two square metres for me. I rolled it up and carried it out under my arm. I could feel the back of it against my bare forearm. I thought I'd lose my mind. The minute I got home, I spread it out on the bathroom floor, like a bath mat. I took a shower and didn't even dry off before I lay down on it. I rolled around, rubbed back and forth. I couldn't stop. The sensation is difficult to describe. I fell asleep there, exhausted. It was a voluptuous sleep, full of green dreams.

When I woke up this morning the whole right side of my body was tattooed with the pattern of miniscule needles. I ran a finger over my skin, feeling the ridges. The blades of grass rustled under the soles of my feet when I stood up.

Now that I sleep alone, the sheets always have the same smell: my smell. There are no olfactory nuances to waft from the pillow as I fall asleep. There are no body hairs, or dead skin cells from someone else's body.

The sheets. Big rectangles of cotton, or linen, or silk, or organza, or satin. Of fur. Yes, I've had sheets custom-made out of pale pink fake fur. It's soft like a baby's blanket. I use them in the winter, obviously, and the dreams I have between those sheets are misty and full of light. Like walking barefoot on the soft dunes of a desert with sunspots blinding my eyes.

I usually put different covers on the pillows. I like to have alternative sensations close at hand, in case I'm restless or wake up during the night.

I have rubber sheets too. Thin rubber, like a latex condom minus the unpleasant smell of lubricant. When I wake up, it feels like my skin is still asleep, numb. And it takes a while before that sensation goes away. It's a little like when your leg falls asleep and you don't feel anything at first and then there's a sudden painful rush of pins and needles.

I also meditate on the state of the world. Yes. Because the world seems better.

There are those who talk about the past and say, After the war we had nothing, we made cigarettes from discarded butts we picked off the pavement, and we didn't have anything to eat but potatoes and polenta, two eggs, and that was fine . . . but what flavours! What eggs! . . . The flavours of once upon a time. Not like the eggs we have now, hatched from factory chickens who feed on rubbish day and night. Those were real eggs, with a big bright yellow yolk. And the pickles on the roadside stalls – big, juicy pickles! And the vegetables back then tasted like the earth and the sun, not like pesticides . . . The bread was home-made; the housewives kneaded the dough themselves . . .

I can't stand people who talk like that. Pesticides, additives, artificial colouring, preservatives are good in food. It's the intelligence of man applied to flavour. I was born alongside Nutella, and it would never occur to me to say that Nutella doesn't taste like chocolate. Nutella *is* chocolate. The same way that artichokes from a jar and tuna from a can *are* real. The artichokes my grandmother makes with oil are disgusting by comparison.

And then there are smells. The exact science of smell is fascinating. They've done unbelievable studies using chemicals to replicate smells precisely; and they keep getting better at it. The formula gets more abstract and more precise at the same time. They give a real idea of taste – they become taste-idea. Banana yogurt, for example, has a flavour that no real banana can ever have.

It's BANANA FLAVOUR. The abstraction: ULTIMATE BANANA.

Yes, the world is better today. There are many things and things keep you company. Things never abandon you. You can buy things; you can keep them, use them, throw them away when they're used up, and buy more. If you're depressed you can go out and buy something – you can buy anything. You can choose it, touch it, have it wrapped up and carry it out of the shop in your bag or in your bare hands. You can unwrap it slowly and look at it for as long as you want. Things aren't jealous. You can have as many of them as you want, and you can put them all next to each other, use them simultaneously: they don't get offended.

Today's world is full of things, and it's better. Starting from a group of base elements, mankind has worked through all the possible combinations and now there are billions of things you can have. Billions of things made out of different materials. If you use up a thing, a product, you can buy more. Unless they take the thing you were regularly using off the market, in which case you just have to have the courage to change, experiment. They might put out a similar version right away, or maybe even a new improved version. You just try something different, make a change. Things can be found everywhere. These days, you don't need to make a special trip, or wait until you have a particular need for something. Just go out, go to the supermarket, walk the aisles with an open mind and you'll find something that's just right for you.

Of course, if you live in a really remote area, and there's only a small local shop nearby, then you must make do with what's there. I get out of places like that as fast as I can. I only go where there are lots of things. To where I can easily find something to satisfy my needs, something to make me feel whole.

It's a better world today.

Over the past few days, though, I've grown bored. I keep needing something different, something new. My skin is losing its sensitivity. It keeps needing stronger things. I want something that flows over me – but not just water, or even another liquid. I need something denser, something that resists the flow, that gathers and swells before slowly dripping down in rivulets. Serpentine.

I have bought some cans of paint. Acrylic colours, very bright resilient colours. The shop assistant brushed the paint over a white surface so I could admire it better. I selected three different ones: *carmine red*, *geranium pink* and a *china blue* which I bought more for its name than anything else, because it's really just a normal electric blue, or even more of a Greek blue than a China blue, like they use on the shutters and doors in Crete.

Anyway, the colours aren't all that important. The consistency is what I was interested in. They're dense but not too dense. Thick and creamy. Velvety.

I also chose an artificial-bristle brush with a big wide base.

I started with *carmine red*. The first stroke was long and straight all the way down my right thigh. I dipped the brush into the can, let the paint soak in and then, without letting it drip, I moved from the top of my thigh down to the bottom very slowly, hardly putting any pressure on the bristles, the tips swollen with colour barely touching me.

I felt cool, almost cold, as the strip of paint gathered into thick heavy rivulets on my skin then dripped down over the crook of my knee. I straightened my leg to help its descent. I worked up to the crease in my groin, then over to my other leg and on to my arm. And my neck, throat, toes, buttocks, knees, every surface of my body, my face too – but I did that in *China blue*, and I painted my stomach *geranium pink*.

As the paint dried I experienced the various stages of the process at different points on my body, from chilly and wet to slightly damp, to the final burning when it's dry.

At this point the burning became intolerable – a kind of diffuse itch – and I got into the shower. My skin was red and painful, covered with blisters and sores, but it was beautiful. I felt real pleasure. And I kept feeling it as I rubbed myself down, using an entire bag of cotton wool, to clean off the last residue of paint.

The paint was great. But it wasn't enough. I feel as though I'm falling, that my perversion will finish me. I feel sucked dry. I need to invent something new, something explosive. Something strong enough to satisfy me for ever. And I'm tired. Today, when I was at Tre Frecce in Corte Isolani having my aperitif, I saw two people kissing. They seemed to like it, to find it strong enough. They kept at it, like kissing was the most ecstatic feeling in the world. The most beautiful. I might have had that same expression on my face the night I got pleasure from my synthetic grass, or between my special sheets, or from just testing the heat of the wide plate on my transparent surfer-blue Rowenta iron, or when my body was covered with acrylic paint. But I don't feel that any more. I'm just tired. As if I've already felt everything there is to feel. Weary repetition without surprise, without some cognitive stimulation to pursue. Everything is too much effort; you need too much patience. The patience to find the right things, to search them out, to test them. Over these last few days, I have no more patience.

It took a week. I hit every pharmacy in the city. They won't give you very much at a time, just a little phial, enough to burn off a wart. Some people asked to see it, but I demurred, saying it would be inconvenient to reveal it in public.

I've lined up all the phials on the bathroom shelf, which I cleared of other objects: vases, bottles, cups, jars. Now, there are only phials there – all white with a black label that reads choleric acid. There are a couple of pale blue ones too. Transparent.

I look at them. I look at them in the morning while I'm getting dressed, in the evening when I'm brushing my teeth. I look at them and get that sucking feeling in my stomach that is simultaneously desire and exhaustion. I have then, before my eyes, the most powerful sensation of my life. A journey, yes, and then when it's over, everything that I've known, tasted, enjoyed, I'll never be able to feel again in the same way. It's a beautiful sensation; it's strong enough. I prolong it. For the moment, I'm waiting, for as long as the sucking feeling lasts. As soon as that starts to fade, I'll take action.

I really like the idea that the surfaces of my body can melt, break, open up and finally consume themselves. It's the same end that all things come to, sooner or later.

The Angel Girl

I didn't want any flowers, I only wanted
To lie with my hands turned up and be utterly empty.

Sylvia Plath, 'Tulips'

It's the same light every morning. No matter what the season. No matter if it's raining, if it's sunny, or if there's a thick fog crowding the streets and blocking the east artery road that I take from my village to the city.

As I walk down the corridor and focus on the black-and-white chessboard linoleum, I am already in the process of preparing myself for the light. I erase shadows from my mind, I keep my eyes lowered, I try to forget everything, try to avoid any possible visual distraction, so that I am ready to enter that perfect realm of definitive light.

When I get to the door, I pause for a fraction of a second, then I push down on the horizontal handle and reach my arm forward into the room to flip the central circuit to the right of the door. The light hits everything at once. Powerful, substantial illumination from brilliant white halogen lamps. It gleams off the icy surfaces of the operating tables and the equipment, off the bare walls and the instruments lined up on the metal shelves. Off the tiled floor.

There's no window. For the light must be consistent. There are no atmospheric variables here. The temperature is regulated by a computerised climate control.

It's always the same. Every single object is always in the exact place it's supposed to be. This is an independent and organised universe. It's mine. I wanted it, I fought to get financing, I designed it, I built it.

There is no other place in the world that could offer the same kind of objective perfection – of serenity minus time. Truth is here inside, and nowhere else. Leaving here at night is like launching yourself out into the darkness, into the numbness of daily life, with its desperate, asyntactical chaos. Chaos: the absence of any regulating principle. That over which I don't have the slightest power. I only have a sense of what I know how to do and what I understand when I'm here in the hospital.

I imagined this light long ago, when I was still a little boy. I sat at a table, hunched over a huge anatomy textbook, and all around me there was a light, so white and impenetrable it cancelled out the slightest variations in the day. Science was a world apart: where day-to-day boredom and the petty stuff of existence were banished. There were only abstractions that formed shapes with every semblance of perfection. A new discovery exploded the shapes, but in an infinitesimal fraction of a second they recomposed themselves into forms even more apparently perfect and luminous than before.

This picture of me seen from behind, my head bowed low over the textbook, was to stay with me for years, though I never shared it with anyone. That image was my antidote to boredom, and the unhappiness that I felt in certain periods. A kind of secret garden tucked away in the corner of my mind, ready to erase everything and restore true life to me. It was a fast-acting drug, a flash meditation.

I've always considered myself an honest man, a hard man on occasion, but generous. Time and again, I've done what needed to be done – that's what I was thinking in the kitchen as I spooned coffee into the filter of the coffee machine. There was a copy of yesterday's newspaper stained with sauce and my mobile on the table.

The ring startled me. I spilled a little coffee on the counter and on the floor, then I cleared my throat and picked up the phone.

A gust of cold wind came in through the open window. It's about to rain, I thought as I said hello. It was one of those early autumn days that make you want to play sick and stay at home in your pyjamas, lolling on the bed, watching leaves through the window and listening to the rain fall.

But then it might just be better to face this day, go out into it, for it won't be different from any other, I thought. It's better than staying in and running the risk of falling asleep. Then the nightmares take over – they're especially bad when you sleep during the day.

I often take a pill to get to sleep at night. I try lying quietly on the bed. I close my eyes and imagine something relaxing. A cornfield, for example, swaying and shimmering in the sunset; the shadows lengthening, and not a sound for miles over the flat countryside. Then the corn and the shadows take sudden form; they rise and turn into strange mutant beings. Their bodies are deformed, their faces are melted, and their eyes empty. I try to squash them. I try to drive them back where they came from. I kick at them. Sometimes it works. Sometimes. But more often it doesn't and I feel like I'd only have to stretch my foot out a few centimetres before I'd be there among them. Sometimes, and only sometimes, I let the lead that ties me to them drag me, weightless and empty, to the other side. Because that's my zone. A world in which I have a purpose. The only one. When that happens, I get out of bed, because I know I won't be able to sleep now. One point five milligrams of Lorazapam would send me into a kind of torpor not unlike sleep. Two point five milligrams would put me to sleep for real. But I don't want to sleep any more.

I turn on all the lights and get into my shirt and boxer shorts. I look around. The rooms in my house are empty and silent. The artificial lights throw serpentine shadows on to the walls. They all look like the creatures of the dark. I smoke a cigarette, drink an iced Nescafé, and finish dressing. The only place I can go now is the hospital.

I drive quickly, hands tight on the cool steering wheel, the night dark and velvet around me, the stars winking brightly. Headlights behind me like sad eyes. I press the accelerator and the wheels skid on the soft asphalt. Inside the car, the voices of Debussy's sirens fill the darkness.

The day he came to find me.

A great deal of time had passed. Years. I don't know how many – something like ten or twelve. He must have been following my career in the newspapers or medical journals. He knew everything about me, my research, my achievements and the history of my hospital.

I looked at him for a long time before recognising him. I couldn't associate his face with any particular moment in my life. It floated before me as if in a murky liquid where the decomposed features of every person I'd ever known, or seen, and never seen again gradually dissolved. I studied his features. His mouth, eyes, cheekbones. That did it. I recognised the cheekbones – they were hard but held the suggestion of a smile, as if they were just about to burst. And then it all came flooding back to me: my first year of university in Bologna, our regular table in the bar, our flushed faces reflecting in the mirror over the table, the heat of the crowd and the alcohol. We're talking about our research. Plans.

He'd never graduated – I couldn't remember why not.

I offered him coffee, tea, a cognac; finally, I offered him a glass of water. He refused it all; he didn't want anything. He looked over my shoulder at a poster on the wall: tiny computer diagrams illustrating the progressive deterioration caused by liver cancer.

He tapped his finger on the ice-blue surface of my desk. His fingernails were chewed down to the skin and his shirt cuffs were frayed.

These signs of neglect were painfully indicative of an unhappy and complicated life. He'd never really known what he wanted. He thought he knew at the beginning; then, one fine day, he didn't know any more. Maybe he suddenly realised he wasn't going to achieve his ambitions, that he didn't have enough talent, or, more importantly, enough commitment. It's not easy to become a real doctor. It's a long, slow road and sometimes you want to flee and forget all about it because everything you've learned will never be enough.

He talks and talks. I think. His words slide over me, thick and sticky – ungraspable. There's a faint trail through them that I just manage to follow, but can't understand.

Then he stops and gets to his feet. The adjustable leather armchair he was sitting on bobs on its springs for a moment after he gets up. I look at, but don't see, the stiff line of his spine. I see him looking out of the window at the trees in the garden, the white path that leads to the front gate.

There's a moment of disjunction between the words racing out from between his lips and my comprehension of them. I take a moment to adjust, so that I can listen in sync with his voice.

You have to help me.

I don't respond. I'm waiting for his request to solidify – to take a real shape. I won't accept this inarticulate wail.

You have to help me. I don't know who else to ask.

I wait. And he turns. His face has fallen; it doesn't look one bit like the face I just retrieved from the pit of my memory.

I look at him. My hands are open on my lap, my arms are loose – it's a posture that's meant to say, Here I am, I'm here.

Who knows if he can read it. I have the impression he's looking at some horrible scene that I can't see.

Wait a second, OK? Calm down, and sit down, please.

I push the chair closer to him, and nod that he should sit down. Though maybe it's more of an order than an invitation. All my uncertainties, my digressive wavering between memories and impressions, disappear. His plea for help has entered me, like a long steel needle penetrating my skull. I'm there. Icy and determined. I'm a doctor again, that and nothing more. I'm curious, even if my curiosity is cold and impersonal. Cruel, even.

He gestures at the leather briefcase he placed on my desk when he first came in; I hadn't even noticed it.

I watch his ratty hands shuffle through the sheaves of paper and card folders to find something – newspaper clippings slide out and fall to the carpet. I kneel down to help him gather his things, but he brushes me away.

No, no. Leave it be. I'll do it . . .

I sit back down on the other side of the desk.

I wait.

Hands clasped under my chin, eyes closed. I don't think of anything. I wait.

Here it is, here.

His voice is like the dry sound the plastic folder makes when he tosses it down on the desk – halfway between us. I open my eyes. His right hand is sitting on top of the folder, as if to keep it still, as if it would fly away or explode if he so much as lifted a finger.

We looked into each other's eyes. His were red and swollen, crossed with flashes of fear.

I reached out towards his hand, still and heavy like a block of stone. I tapped the back of his hand with my index finger.

Take your hand away. Let me see.

He yanked his arm back like a frightened child, but then he didn't seem to know where to put it. I noticed the anguished hesitation in his movement.

I pulled the folder towards me. I opened it.

Two large-format photographs of the same subject. Two close-up portraits in black and white.

The subject was a very young girl. She had a peculiar face, thin and hollow, but also curvaceous. Her full mouth was pale. Her eyes wore an uncertain expression, gentle but profound. She seemed to be looking past real things to an invisible world – beyond the photographer's lens, the photographer himself, beyond the backdrop, the day that found her sitting there, under strong, unnatural lights.

I lifted my eyes to look at him, but saw that he was looking down at the photos. I thought they must look strange upside down. I flipped the page.

It was the same girl, but these were full-length portraits. Her body had the same untenable quality her face had; it was slender and elastic, her muscles were long and delineated. Her ribs stuck out in a perfect arcade, one after the other, the effect made even more striking under the shiny fabric of her one-piece swimsuit. You could almost read the whiteness of her bones.

She was on the next page too. But if I hadn't already known it was her, I wouldn't have recognised her. Her slight body was naked. She seemed like the stem of a long flower, bending in the breeze. Her skin was pale, an uncommon fierce white. Like she'd been pumped with white lead and it had spread over her like a second skin. A thick, tight sheath that followed every tiny fold and dip of her body.

Her eyes were encircled with black powder, which made them sink deeply into her face, totally different from the face in the first photos. Her eyes had no expression, they were two dark poisonous wells. Her hands flanked the side of her face, covering her ears. Her mouth was wide open: a pale pink hole rimmed with tiny, uneven teeth.

I looked up. He was there, sitting stiffly on the edge of his chair, his shoulders and chin leaning towards me.

Who is it?

Please keep looking. I beg you. Look first, and then I'll explain.

I nodded, without looking away from his clear, desperate eyes.

I turned another page.

This time I had to force myself not to cry out.

The girl was curled into a ball, legs and arms all wrapped up. A deflated ball of white flesh. Her head was hidden between her shoulders. You could just see her back. It was narrow, long and bony. Over her shoulder blades two wings, like bat wings, opened out. They looked like they were made of skin held up by tiny sticks that were bowing under the weight. Underneath, open wounds, red and glossy. It looked like the skin had just been cut out and lifted up. You could see the live flesh, the red lines, and rows of tiny, taut muscles and raw nerves.

Can you please.

I beg you I beg you I beg you.

His voice was a running mumble, like water in a stream or flowing from an open tap.

I leafed through the remaining photos quickly, without making comment. I was moved. The face and body that had initially struck me as lovely and fragile gradually became something else, assuming contours that left the human shape a distant memory. It was a body transformed according to the most horrendous dreams. Nightmares made flesh.

I still couldn't work out if it was all a matter of trickery. My hands had started trembling and I was not nearly as removed as I had felt initially. He didn't speak; he just kept looking at me with that stunned expression that made me feel even more confused.

I shut the folder and put my hand on it. I tapped my fingers for a moment, then stopped. I forced myself to assume that impenetrable expression that seems to so comfort the sick.

Who is it?

You saw the clippings at the back too?

I opened the folder at the back. There were lots of them, folded and refolded into tiny squares, in every language.

The angel girl, they read. The angel girl and her flesh wings.

I looked at my hands. They are big and strong, not at all what you'd expect of a surgeon's hands, which are often described with the same language as concert pianists' – long and steady, with slender, elegant fingers – elastic, fluid. My hands have none of these qualities. They are solid, energetic; they are peasant hands, or perhaps a sculptor's hands, able to manipulate matter without getting hurt. They always know exactly the right pressure to use, how to maintain a constant balance between force and delicacy.

Every crevice, fold and wrinkle of my hands preserves the memory of a shattered face, or a limb torn apart by bullets or a land mine, of skin corroded by acid or illness. Under the pads of my fingers I can still feel the fibres of flesh, the temperature of blood gushing from a cut artery. The indescribably soft skin of a newborn baby that has just stopped breathing. My hands. My big, strong hands have sewn up, pieced together, transformed, and turned horror into decency, made ugliness at least tolerable.

My hands remember everything. My eyes forget. They erase, annul, paste a thick, black coating over every image. My ears, too, have forgotten every moan, every complaint, every scream.

I made him a coffee. I put the cup in front of him and added sugar without even asking him if he took it that way. In the meantime I kept thinking, and memories flooded out of my fingers. Every movement I made became a grating memory. It all came back: faces and places forgotten years ago. Makeshift operating rooms set up in the middle of a battle-torn field, among the whistling bullets and the cries of people trying to flee. The sleepless nights crouching under a bunk bed, or in a tiny room, as drafty and austere as a monk's cell.

Who is it? I mean, to you. For you – who is she?

It was clear from the way his chin and cheeks were shaking that the words were exploding on his tongue, but he couldn't force them out. They sat there, locked inside his mouth, like dead insects. He shut his eyes halfway and tried to recover the minimum of calm he needed to talk to me. Then, all in one breath, he said, She's Angela, my sister.

The corners of her mouth were cut away to reveal her gums, and her tiny teeth had been filed down to almost nothing.

Her back was the masterpiece. Or rather, it had once been the masterpiece. The angel wings were now just two dangling flaps of skin, frayed like an old shirt. The skin under them was shiny and pearled, so thin you could see the lines and fibres of her tendons and muscles underneath.

I studied her from a distance. She was reclining on one side, and so in order to get a complete picture, I had to walk around her as if she were a statue. In fact the way she was lying made her look quite like the *Hermaphrodite* in the Louvre.

Despite what she had done to her eyelids, her eyes were vibrant. They were dark and shiny like fish eyes. They watched me without changing expression – without the light in them changing. They darted around the room, following my movements.

I kept my hands in the pockets of my coat. They were trembling. My lips were trembling too, but I clenched my teeth and sucked in my cheeks.

She watched me. Her gaze was like that of an animal in the zoo or in the windows of a pet shop. Curious but distant and lost at the same time, in a silent world where there is no fear or trembling. Lost in a world of constraint without emotion.

I drew near to her, touched one cheek and she didn't pull away. She let my fingertips slide over her scars.

The strong light of the lamps reflected off the deteriorated scales of her skin. She was like a big fish, breaded and ready to be tossed into boiling oil.

Hers was a look I had seen many times before without it affecting me – on buses, in the street, in supermarkets, on advertising hoardings, or floating out from the shiny pages of fashion magazines.

But her look was more naked, and she was looking right at me.

Her body was much thinner than it had looked in the pictures. Smooth and white, all tendon and muscle: she had no fat accumulation whatsoever, not even that little bit that makes a woman womanly. Her breasts were flat rounds, vague suggestions of flesh over a prickly plain of bones and sharp edges.

As I circled her, my anxiety quickened and I shook. I had many thoughts. I thought about what I wanted to do. About what I wanted to show the world. I thought of others like her. And my fingertips began to remember. They quivered and I felt them flood with forgotten stories and faces. I felt again under my fingertips the consistency of skin that was swollen and reddened from accidents and illness, the final beat of a heart vomited out of the crushed chest cavity of an Israeli soldier. While the black night over our heads exploded into red fire.

I made everyone, the nurses and assistants, leave the room. We were left alone. The light in that room seemed brighter than ever. It was a universe of light, enclosed within these four naked walls, a universe of thoughts pounding in my head, keeping beat with my heart. Blood and images, memories and that sense of urgency pumped through me. Hurry. Hurry up.

I put the anaesthesia mask over her mouth, checked her blood pressure, monitored her heart.

Her fish eyes locked on to mine. Silent. Indifferent. Then, they closed, and the scars on her face fashioned another expression over the real one. Like an ancient statue: still and impassive. I put my hand over her eyes. I took her face between my palms and squeezed it, the way you do with someone you love. And then the urgency mounted. Hurry.

Hurry up.

This sudden alacrity came out of nowhere, a secret ability I'd never be able to explain. It was instinct more than anything else: what ability becomes when it's part of you.

The light was bright and white. My hands were quick and steady.

Cries, screams of pain, explosions resounded in my head. Each incision, each clean cut echoed.

And for the first time, it all took the right shape.

She woke up, and her eyes were tired. The sockets were dark and sunken. Her mouth was dry.

   She looked at me for a long time before being able to focus. That happens to everyone. I waited. I sat in front of her and watched her fish eyes warm and come to life.

   Then I waited for her to look down at her self.

   She said but one word and it wasn't what I would have expected. Maybe, I hadn't expected anything because I knew whatever she said would shock me.

Finally.

Her head fell back and her eyes assumed the statue-like expression. Her empty, breathless body was like one of the dummies we use for resuscitation training.

   I touched her with my fingers sheathed in surgical rubber: the exposed viscera, the red-raw skin, inside out. I felt the white, shiny ribs, curved outwards like an exotic clothes rack, her rubbery little uterus, empty, pink and tender, like a freshly cleaned cuttlefish.

   I covered her with a sheet and turned out the lights.

   It was darkest night and all the rush had disappeared. The sounds in my head stopped hurting. There were only Debussy's sirens singing like the wind on the sea.

Two of Us

And since that winter I have learnt to gaze
on life indifferently as through a pane of glass.

Derek Walcott, 'A Village Life'

Since then, when the sky turns this colour, my heart beats more quickly, and it all comes back to me.

I saw her for the first time on a winter morning. The sky was white, like today, and the branches of the trees were naked.

She wore a red quilted jacket. Red against the day's white background. It seemed like a good sign.

I looked at her face last. First, the jacket, then, her legs. They're not good legs. They're heavy and she has thick ankles. She was wearing leather boots with a fur lining that stuck out over the top. Old-lady winter shoes.

I am standing at the bus stop in front of the hospital. I stamp my feet on the ground to warm them, clench my hands tightly into fists and bury them in my pockets.

Our eyes meet. Her gaze is a dark flash. She has enormous, ferocious, steady eyes. She looks at me. It's definitive from the first moment. It must have been that current racing through my bones.

Bus number 25 arrived. She got on. I didn't. I waited for another one.

Stupid, I think. You should have got on and followed her. But I was nailed to the spot out of habit.

I didn't think of anything else the whole day. That red jacket, her flashing dark eyes, that current.

I had to wait because she wasn't there the next morning, or for the rest of the week. Then I saw her again. It was another white morning and I immediately recognised her red jacket from a distance as I walked up to the bus stop with my mouth buried in my scarf.

We talked, sure, but I can't remember who initiated the conversation.

I invited her to dinner. We met at the bus stop. I felt uneasy, worried I'd see someone I knew, worried about them seeing me with a woman who was not very attractive. A sleight of words to avoid saying 'ugly'.

I told her I preferred to eat somewhere out of town. Saturday-night crowds bothered me and I knew a place with good food and a quiet atmosphere. She didn't say anything. She climbed into the car.

She didn't speak to me as I drove. She kept her head turned to the window, looking out. She watched the fields, which were almost invisible under dense fog, the houses, the street lamps. She seemed perfectly at ease, as was I. There was nothing to say: just the two of us, a man and a woman journeying across foggy countryside, two people on their way somewhere.

The fog suddenly lifted and the road opened up in front of us, dark and glistening. I sped up. A small shadow shot out in front of the car, I tried to brake, clutching the steering wheel to keep from swerving, but I couldn't control it.

The inability to take risks is something we all have written into us. Almost all of us. It's an attachment to life that keeps us from killing in cold blood. I was angry at myself, and overcome by a chilling nausea.

I can't distinctly reconstruct the chain of events: I was upside down, my legs locked and my right arm wedged under her, handling all that flesh. We were in a pit and everything around us was silent and far away.

You're scared to kill a cat . . . You swerved to keep from hitting it . . .

There was a strange, dark, poisonous edge to her voice. It was as if someone had slapped me. I didn't answer, but I felt a burning inside.

The first time came a month later. It was February and the night was clear and starry. Every evening we'd go walking through the Chinese quarter, over by the racecourse. We both liked that neighbourhood, the way it suddenly made you feel as if you were somewhere else, in another place, in another city. Any other city. The streets were lit with the coloured neon signs of Chinese restaurants and takeaways; we were surrounded by people who couldn't care less about us.

We walked quietly side by side, not holding hands, just periodically brushing each other's sleeves. Suddenly she stopped. She stood still and looked at me. I asked her if there was anything wrong – was she hungry, cold, tired. She kept on staring at me with her eyes flashing cold and mean, slicing right through the lenses of her glasses into my retinas.

I wanted to avert my eyes. I wanted to hide.

With a sudden lurch she raises her hand and grabs my throat. Her fingers are large, clammy and freezing. Her hands don't seem like they belong to a woman. She stiffens. I'm having trouble breathing and there's something inside of me that wants to escape despite everything. I shut my eyes. I don't want to see her. I just want to keep feeling the pressure of her hands and her warm breath on my neck. The weight of her body against mine. I want to keep hiding.

I was paralysed, teetering on the edge of a cliff. I was about to fall – I was convinced of it – and I would never be able to go back to how I was before.

She laughed.

I had been waiting for her. I understand that now. She was what I had been waiting for. All the others, who had come before her, were like bridges. Delicate bridges whose purpose it was to bring me ever closer to her – bridges that would have collapsed the instant she set foot on them.

The city weighed down on us. It was damp and powerful, like a living creature. Even the dark seemed human. It breathed with us. I was frightened, but I sensed she wasn't. She never was, not even for an instant. Her black eyes shone steady and cold. She was what I would have liked to be. But, I've always been too scared. This was the difference between us.

When she squeezed my throat that first time, standing over by the racecourse the night of the full moon, she knew exactly what she was doing.

I go for approximations – like all men. She doesn't. She's a woman, and a plain woman. Her plainness makes her even stronger. She knew everything about me. She knew I was scared. She knew that much right away, from the car accident. She knew what I wanted. And she had been waiting for the moment. Like a vulture, she spotted her prey, hid in the dark shadow of a cloud and, at the right moment, descended on me. She wanted it to come like a bolt out of nowhere. To take me by surprise. I looked at her through misty eyes, looked deep down into her glistening blackness.

She laughed.

It lasted five seconds. We kept on staring at each other, then I closed my eyes and she hugged me, but I know her eyes were still open. I'm sure of it. I'm sure she was looking up at the sky, the still light of the February stars.

Our house.

It was rented, big and empty, on the outskirts of the city. The building was tall and white. There were 110 apartments in it and a large communal garden at the back. It was too big for two people but we needed the space. Neither of us had lived with someone for quite a while. We wanted to be able to walk through rooms without constantly running into each other, without having to share the airspace. There were a lot of empty rooms. It was luminous. That was our favourite thing about it. How bright all the rooms were – so it didn't matter that there was no furniture, except for a bed, a table and a couple of chairs. We'd disposed of all our other stuff. Everything was new. Nothing reminded us of the past.

She left the house before me in the morning. Before she went, she laid out breakfast on the table. Coffee and orange juice. Biscuits. Sometimes, a paper flower. She was good at making paper flowers. Strange thing, with her thick manly fingers.

We would come back every evening at about the same time. That's when life began. Our life together, the real life. We'd talk, but I don't remember about what. We'd talk for hours, never about work or regular things. No, we'd talk about us, about the two of us, together in that house. We almost never turned on the television, and when we did we never paid much attention to it. We'd keep changing the channel. We'd look at the images but we'd be thinking of other things. Every night – always in a different way – we'd come to it. Sex. We did it every night. Sometimes in anger, sometimes with affection. But we'd always do it, and for a long time.

Once, she made me climb on to the kitchen table. I lay there stiffly, almost holding my breath. She sat on me and did it all by herself. Then, without warning, she grabbed my head between her hands and started smashing it against the table.

I almost didn't realise what was happening at first. I had been lying there with my eyes closed, following her hips with mine, then I opened my eyes and saw her face. Her eyes were half closed, her features twisted into a grimace, her teeth were bared, like an animal. I'd seen that expression before, but never on her. I didn't try to free myself. I waited for whatever had taken hold of her to pass. She kept beating my head against the wood, hard, and she screamed. I raised my arms and grabbed her neck and I squeezed tightly. I threw her to the ground. She landed there on all fours, naked and ugly. That deformed expression was still on her face.

We didn't talk about it. We never talked about it. Up until then, we'd been studying each other, a reciprocal learning process about the other person. Now, a big empty space had been opened up. All barriers were down. We didn't need to talk. She was like me. But maybe we'd known that from the beginning – even if we hadn't been as sure of it as we were now.

After that, we began to do it even more. The affection had disappeared, there was only violence and then calm when it was all over. We'd fall asleep exhausted, each of us on our side of the bed.

Then the girl came. She brought her into our house. She said we needed the money and the house was so big that even renting out a room we wouldn't notice there was someone else. I disagreed. Our solitary, wild evenings would be limited: volume down, only in the bedroom. But I didn't say anything. She had made the decision. It had always been her. I changed my mind about the whole thing when I saw the girl. She was beautiful. I liked to watch her while I was drinking my morning coffee. I liked to run into her at the door when I was coming home. She worked as a waitress in a club and stayed home all day, sleeping and reading magazines that she left scattered everywhere. Stupid magazines, filled with horoscopes and beauty treatments. But she was pretty. She was slender and wore her blond hair cropped short; it fell in wisps over the back of her neck. She had a neck like a child. I liked to watch her from behind when she warmed the milk on the stove – for my coffee too. She reminded me of someone. A child I knew when I was a child. And she had a beautiful smile, gracious and easy like a sunburst.

Once I brushed against her. She didn't pull away. She seemed to want it. It happened just like that, not a word exchanged between

us. It was quick. She had long legs and a smooth body. But she
didn't know how to do anything; she was just like a baby.

She saw it right away, that evening, when the three of us were at
home together. One glance was enough – to pick up on the girl's
embarrassment and on my fear. But she just smiled. Her hyena
smile, stormy and cruel. I realised that she'd wanted it to happen.
She'd brought the girl into the house precisely in order to make it
happen.

I lowered my head, as always.

She knew where we were going.

One Saturday night the girl had a fever and stayed home from
work. She curled up on the couch in front of the television, a
blanket over her legs and her eyes red and shiny. She was lovely all
the same, and seemed even younger. I couldn't stop looking at her
and she smiled.

We ate without speaking. The atmosphere was constricted, as if
we were in suspension. It felt like time had become glued into this
one dense, deep moment that seemed to last a year. Infinite. It was
dark outside and inside the house. Just the light of the television
and the flickering candle on the table. Headlights from the cars on
the road that passed under our window.

She kept looking at the girl. Quick glances between bites of food.
She didn't turn her head, just flashed her gaze over to the form
curled up on the couch, then retracted her eyes immediately. She
ate slowly with a blank expression on her face. It was the first time
we had all been together this way. It was strange.

After dinner, I started clearing the table. I put the plates in the
sink and filled it with soapy water. I like washing up. I rub my
fingers over the cold slippery surfaces and don't think of anything.
She was sitting next to the girl. They sat in silence, their eyes glued
to the television. There was one of those Saturday-evening variety
shows on, with dancers and comedians. The volume was low and I
don't think they were paying too much attention. Every so often I'd

turn to look at them. She kept sliding closer to the girl, and the girl didn't move away. Slowly, she edged over until the two of them were sitting shoulder to shoulder, hip to hip. I heard the faint whisper of their breath and the music from the variety show. When I finished washing up, I dried my hands on the towel, turned off the tap and turned around. She had one hand wrapped tightly around the girl's throat. That delicate, slender throat was completely encircled by those thick man's hands. I don't remember what I felt. Maybe excitement, but I was scared too.

I didn't say anything. Time had again condensed into a single deep black moment and no words came out of my mouth.

I should have stopped her.

I should have, but I didn't.

I moved closer. And it started like this. Slowly and clumsily in the dark. Imperceptible movements dragged us on top of each other before either one of us had a chance to choose, to decide.

Night stopped. It was squashed between two pieces of paper, stiff with glue, like the lifeless body of a butterfly.

The girl's legs were wrapped around my hips. Her hands were wrapped around the girl's neck.

It was dark. I kept my eyes clenched shut to keep it that way. It was all so silent. The girl's eyes were wide open, and bright like a doll's eyes in the dark. Like enamel. Her spread legs were a sandy, sweet inlet. I believe I might have fallen asleep in there, resting on that cool sand.

She didn't say anything. She got up, took my hand and led me to bed. She tucked the blankets in around me and rubbed my forehead like a mother. She shut the door behind her and I fell fast asleep. I didn't dream of anything. I didn't think of anything. I slept. A deep, quiet sleep, all black.

She returned.

I don't know what time it was, but it must have been almost dawn. There was a chilly purple light filtering into the room.

She was sweating. Her shirt clung to her body. The dampness brought out shades of purple and red in the white material, like the early morning sky. She undressed quickly, letting her clothes drop to the ground. I averted my eyes the way I always do. A flash: her big oblong breasts, the equine power of her hips. She sat on the edge of the bed and reached out towards me. I smelled the bitter scent of her skin mixed with something else, sweeter and more complex. It was the girl's smell, but more complicated than I remembered. She slid on top of me, as she usually did. She pushed her head into my shoulder, dug her teeth into my skin and put me in her. She moved quickly, taking my sex and holding me tightly between her thighs. Her weight pinned me to the bed. I could taste her thick frizzy hair between my lips. She didn't say anything. I didn't say anything.

I inhaled the girl's smell from her hair. Sweet.

It was over instantly. She shook, three or four contractions, and then she collapsed back on to the bed. She fell asleep. I stayed there, watching her breasts rise and fall with her breath. Quiet. I tried to sleep too. I tried to find a good position, to think of something relaxing – a quiet landscape, for example. The sea. Trees bending gently. Something slow and silent. But I was overwhelmed with desire. I smelled the girl's sweet scent. I saw her throat, her blonde hair, her long slender legs, her pointy little breasts.

The sweet scent of her body. Sweet.

I got up and left the room.

It was almost dawn. The house was blazing with phosphorescent purples and blues. The light lengthened shapes, spread over the walls like paint. The kitchen floor felt funny beneath my feet. There was some plastic sheeting on the ground. My bare feet almost slid out from under me. My pyjama trousers whispered with every step.

The room was sweet with perfume.

The whole house was.

It was a perfume I remembered from childhood, from distant days, unfocused yet vividly imprinted on my cells. Like memories always are – hidden deeply away in fractions of our cells. Pus trapped in a pore, ready to explode with the slightest pressure.

Something I hadn't thought about for a very long time came to mind.

My mother.

My mother left at dawn. A dawn just like this. The sky was white and the windows of the house were wide open but still the smell wouldn't go away. It lurked in the corners, sticking like a film to the walls and covering the furniture and the upholstery.

I walked through the rooms, ran through them, one after the other, my arms spread wide, playing aeroplane.

Children do stupid things like that.

A shimmering plane flying high over a city in flames. Dropping silent bombs. I whistled. The others stood around her in silence, their faces long. My sister was crying and my father was holding one of my mother's wrists between his hands. That's what they told me. My eyes were closed. I inhaled the sweet air and let it glide over me like an embrace. I flew fast over the smoking ruins of a dead city.

The smell was the same that morning. I shut my eyes tightly in the middle of the kitchen. I moved cautiously. I spread my arms to see what effect it had. For a moment I felt as if I was an aeroplane shooting through the white sky. For a moment.

Then her hand was on my shoulder. I turned to her but kept my eyes shut. Her smell was even stronger. It was bitter like berries on a pine tree.

It's early, she said.

I nodded.

I'll make breakfast. Are you hungry?

I nodded again.

She touched my cheek. Her fingers were warm and smelled of soap.

Holding our coffee mugs, we sat in front of the window and watched the dawn. The sun rose over the horizon, icy and white. It was a pure light, the colour of the girl's body.

It was deepest winter. A morning like this.

Nocturne

I turn off the light
my heart a cliff
before the moon

Kato Shuson, 'Haiku'

First Night

I've only been alone for one day, and already everything is different. The house is unfamiliar. The lights that I turn on and off are filters that alter the image. I have total control over the outcome of each flick.

Houses: you live in them and forget all about how they're made. They don't belong to anyone when they're being shared: zones have functions and different atmospheres, the movements of the inhabitants overlap and create confusion. Months pass before you remember the existence of a room, or a particular chair, or window, or the possibility of using every square inch of space.

You forget the unique silence of an empty house. The swinging doors and creaking wood during the night. The empty spaces, the corners where you can curl up like a baby. The coolest spots in the middle of the summer. The cool linoleum on the kitchen floor, the fan running at full speed over you.

Your perception of time changes too. When you're alone you can eat whenever you want, walk around the house until dawn, take a shower in the middle of the night. It's a complete upheaval of the

rules that define and structure the days. It can be frightening sometimes: without limits the days stretch and shorten uncontrollably.
The hours lengthen around you and are full of shadows.

I sleep during the day, that's all I do. I drift into sleep towards dawn
and don't wake until the late afternoon. Sometimes I lose track of
time under the combined effect of alcohol, marijuana and sleeping
pills: it's five in the morning and it seems like the onset of the night.
I sleep through the light that filters in through the blinds. Carbon-
paper blue that fades into pale purple.

I keep the sedatives on the shelf in the bathroom. I use a different
one depending on what kind of sleep I want. Sedatives are not all
the same. They have very distinct flavours, recognisable from the
first drop that falls on your tongue and runs down your throat.
Gelatin capsules take longer to kick in. Chalky pills melt the instant
you put them in your mouth. Each one offers a different profundity
of sleep. Some don't even make you sleep, they make you drowsy
instead; they embrace you with warm, pillowy arms. Others bury
you in bed, eliminating all possible contact between your brain and
central nervous system.

When I'm alone, I think there's something waiting for me on
sleep's threshold. Something that wants to take me away to silent,
strange places. Something that waits, and never tires of waiting.
When it takes me, I dream a lot. I dream in colour, I think, though
I forget the colours. I remember the bridge of a ship, storms at sea,
cats, aeroplanes driving down busy city streets. There's always a
great deal of dirty, murky water. Sea. Here, I always dream of the
sea. But I never dream of a limpid, calm sea. There are always
storms, waves washing me away, black water with creatures under
the surface, waiting to catch me.

If I go out at all, it's late. I read, listen to music, take a shower,
water the plants until eleven. Then something clicks and I have

to get out. At night, without some protective presence, my sleep becomes too vast a territory. I'd rather fall asleep stoned, listening to car engines, the birds singing, the neighbours opening their shutters. There's the world again, and I can sleep, with a background of voices and the secure knowledge that things are present around me.

My mother, father, and brother left early without saying goodbye. It must have still been dark out because there was no light coming through the blinds and there was silence – no birds or car engines. Half asleep I heard the gurgle of the coffee machine, steps on the stairs, water running in the bathroom and muffled voices. I didn't have the strength to get up. The door closed and the silence in the house became absolute. I fell back to sleep effortlessly, protected by the dark and the walls of the house which was finally empty.

It's almost seven and the telephone has been ringing all afternoon. I left the answering machine on low volume. I'm sitting on the porch steps. I can feel thin blades of grass and clover under my bare feet and between my fingers. If I turn around, I can see from here the blinking light on the answering machine. A sick little eye, winking to get my attention.

There have been too many men over these last two years. There have been so many that I don't think I remember them all. I just had one date, maybe two with some of them; with others, we were together for several months before I got tired of it. There were times I thought it would last. More often, I didn't even consider that possibility.

In the confusion of different faces, hands and sexual organs, I've forgotten the important things. I don't remember the smile of the man I was with for three years. I know his sex was long and straight and didn't curve; that his erection stood at an angle. That he had a little birthmark by his heart. It's a twin to the one I have on my stomach. But I can't remember his smile.

I thought of him. Reluctantly thinking back on all the beds we slept on, all the absurd places where we did it: the car seats, deserted yards, forests, little churches in the mountains, clearings in olive groves, bushes up rocky hillsides, the parks in the middle of the day – hidden among the trees – hotel rooms, the car park of a ferry, the stairwell of an apartment block, the tables.

All those promises. Promises that slide from lips, as irrepressible and ephemeral as orgasms, that seem to dig deep pits inside you, but are really only fleeting air bubbles.

I thought of our parents, how they too have slept on different beds as they travel the world, legs entwined, a hand seeking out the other's neck, a thin shock of hair clenched between teeth, or caught in the crook of an arm, or leg. The cool length of sheets their bodies converge on, legs first, and then the rest.

His arms, his smooth torso and the birthmark by his heart. His hands. And it's over. Still I can't remember his smile. When exactly did I forget?

His body has become a stranger's body even if I know it better than anyone's. Elusive and mute. Useless. Nothing remains. His voice, too, which I've had so near, I've forgotten. Or rather my heart doesn't know how to perceive it any more. Memories get stuck and overlap. Here, they shimmer; there, they suddenly freeze-frame.

I think this happens to everyone. Memories we don't care about stick – the faces we never loved, the insignificant moments, details, like a wart or a hairy mole – the unpleasant or inessential things just stay there, bright and clear. Indelible. Who knows why.

Now that I am responsible for filling it and emptying it, the refrigerator has also taken on a new identity. I open it and the dim light sweetly floods the room, making me think of the guilty snacks of my adolescence. A plump girl spending restless nights eating anything remotely edible she could put her hands on.

Now that it's mine, I have emptied it all out. I spent the morning checking expiry dates and throwing out sauces, jam, butter, eggs. I cleaned it meticulously, pulling out the fruit and vegetable drawers and scrubbing at the corners. When I saw it standing before me, empty and glistening clean, I felt something that's hard to describe: relief, a sense of order extending from that rectangular box into my head and my guts.

Cleaning often gives this sensation. Especially cleaning the kitchen. It's a sensation of well-being: your head is emptied, the world seems under control and organised. Cookery programmes make me feel the same way. My favourite ones are on the BBC. The images are so neat and clinical. Pots are lined up like surgical instruments on clean counters. The clean vegetables and meat waiting on white plates. The antiseptic voice of the presenter. I like the more basic programmes too. I like to hear those voices listing grammes and calories, and describing the preparation step by step. It makes me feel good. It's like when you're little and you're hanging around the table waiting for your mother to make some food. Watching those automatic and regular movements gives you a sensation of calm, continuity, of order.

You can apply this same method to your friendships – to your sentimental life. Put everyone in a row and see who passes and who doesn't. Some of them might need throwing out. I don't trust the person who says reorganise all the boxes until you have found the right arrangement. Throw things out. The world is too full already. There's too much mess, inside and out.

I think I'll stay by myself tonight. I don't want to go out. I don't want to talk and stay out late. I want to be in this silence, with the lights off, the stereo off, listening to the sounds of the country and the children playing outside.

I count eight messages on the answering machine. I listen to them when I go back into the living room to get a drink and a cigarette. They are mostly men. My grandmother calling to wish me a happy twenty-fourth birthday – my birthday was last month – and men. Friends, ex-lovers, acquaintances. There isn't a single voice that inspires any emotion in me, a shiver of desire or a spark of affection. They are voices. Voices talking to someone who isn't here. Who isn't here any more. Each one of them addresses a me who is no longer to be found. They don't have anything to tell me, I think. We had sex. We probably also laughed together. But none of them left more than an annoying trace on me, like a rash, like skin acting up. Itchy and irritating.

I'm staying alone tonight. I am going to try and be self-sufficient. I have to be able to go on without needing an approving glance.

Second Night

I have turned on all the lights in the house, and the garden lights too. I like to imagine the wheel of the electricity meter whirling and spinning – whirling like me.

I have drunk a couple of glasses of dry white wine. I've smoked a little. I walk around the house, looking in all the mirrors.

Nights like this happen. You want something but you don't know what. A man, any man. You want to hear stupid things whispered in your ear, to be seduced. There are girls who go out looking for these things in nightclubs and bars. They spend hours trying on ridiculous outfits. They put on make-up. They spray perfume all over themselves. They carry condoms and other gadgets in their handbags. I can't do that sort of thing. I'm not like that. You can't see someone properly in the dark, and I need to be sure I'm with someone I really like.

I put on Nick Cave's *Murder Ballads*. P.J. Harvey's warm, dark voice slides through the night and mixes with the dark, rough-as-wool voice of Nick Cave. The song is a sad fairy tale. The story of a love so big and wild it can kill.

Before going upstairs to change, I turn up the volume so the dark suffering voices will follow me around the house.

I put on my pale pink vinyl skirt and shiny, tight, black shirt. Sandals with high heels, without stockings, or knickers. I haven't dressed like this for a long time. I must be in the right mood. Sometimes I'll dress up for a man, but more often I do it for myself. I like the transformation. I see the years on my face under the make-up, and on my body under the clothes. The chrysalis that turns into a butterfly – that old story.

I check myself in the mirror a few more times. My make-up is running because of the heat and so I put powder on my nose, forehead and chin. I watch myself smile, see the relaxation; I part my lips, half close my eyes. I peek at myself through my lowered lashes.

He rang twice. And I waited before letting him in. I turned off all the kitchen lights and watched him through the blinds. I couldn't see the expression on his face, but I could see his big, clumsy silhouette. He was wearing the white hat that he always wears in the summer – his gentleman-poet hat – it makes him look older than he is.

We talked for a while, seated across from each other in the kitchen, eating prawn-cocktail crackers and drinking chilled Chardonnay, followed by some fizzy wine.

When he drinks his eyes get narrow and wet. They seem even paler.

I remember all the times we drank together. All the times I watched his eyes change. All the times we talked and laughed together.

All the times he lifted his hand to touch my hair.

He does what he always does, what everyone would do if they had the courage to ask. He puts his sex on my lips and rolls it around; he's got his other hand tight on the back of my neck so I can't move. Two, three minutes pass, then there's a thick, warm spurt. It slides between my lips and down my chin. I jerk myself free and hold my breath. I try not to swallow. I lock myself in the bathroom and spit, holding my head under the powerful jet of the cold-water tap.

There's nothing to say, really. My white bathrobe wrapped

around my body, I go back into the dark room and look at the outline of his body on the bed. His legs spread, his arms tucked behind his head. I see his eyes shining in the dark. I wish he'd disappear, right now, with a wave of my hand. But I have to wait, until he gets it. Until he notices my lack of interest.

Third Night

I'm watching them, every last one of them: these men who force themselves into my life and presume to telephone me, date me, write letters to me and break me with their love. I watch how they behave in a hostile environment. I listen to their talk. I'm seduced by their gestures. That's what they believe.

They're all different, and yet there's one precise moment, a fraction of a second, in which their faces fuse into a single image.

I line them up like soldiers, all in a row, in matching uniforms, even spaces between each copy; there are no preferences here. I want them neutral and naked in my house. I want to watch them eat, see them use the wrong fork, see them lick their knives, or use the fish knife for meat. I want to observe them carefully, see their lips open and close over awkward syllables. See their lost eyes like an animal in a trap looking back at me because they know that I make the rules here. I decide. It might be all right with me, and it might not be. I want one at a time. One after the other. All of them. The ones I weeded out and discarded without ever looking back; the ones that fled on their own and made me suffer for a while.

It wasn't hard to find him. His number is the same, so is his voice. He's an unchanging man – even the way he answers the telephone, pauses, laughs – it's all the same. How many years have passed? Five, maybe more, maybe seven. I was little when we started. How often was he the one who sought me out on those nights when there weren't any other friends or women for him.

We chatted, compared notes on mutual friends: graduations, marriages, betrayals. We made an appointment for midnight. I was already a bit out of it when I got there – dope, and a little beer. My vision was clouded. The same faces, the usual chaos, the typical back and forth of people who have nothing to do or think about on these summer nights, with the damp heat coming off the plains around the city. I took the long way, around the perimeter of the square, trying to avoid people. I enjoyed feeling eyes upon me, brushing casually against complete strangers. Then I saw him. My heart started beating faster, but my desire passed instantly. I couldn't summon up the calm I needed to look at him. I made an excuse and left. As I left, my high heels slid under me, as if I were walking on ice, and I shut my eyes for a moment to close out the sea of sweaty, smiling faces.

Fourth Night

I've heard what men say about a woman's sex and it gives me the shivers. They might feel the same if they heard a woman commenting on length and hang. We're all contained in that tiny zone of our bodies, the centre, where everything takes shape. Life manifests itself from there. The origin of the world, like that secret painting by Courbet.

A woman's sex distends with pregnancy, changes with age, dries up.

Every time a man has entered me, I've felt shivers running through me. I was frightened. A fear so violent that the mere thought of my body changing made me double over with nausea.

My first lover had to keep trying for a while to make my sex open. He had to prepare me, with his fingers and tongue, and each time he got a little further inside me. After a month of trying, it worked. The TV was on, the lights were off: the gunshots of cowboys and horses' hoofs, the rounding up of herds. He suddenly slid in. And then I changed. From that moment I listened to what he said, and every time he was in me I alternated between being pleased and horrified.

Every time we speak of sex we touch the deepest and most hidden place in our bodies. Measurements, commentary, calculations all annihilate something, even if you can't get away from them.

When I look at a man's sex, I feel neither dislike, nor rancour. I can only feel compassion.

I'm alone tonight too, and I think I did the right thing to leave yesterday. It wouldn't have done any good to make love to him again. To let him take my body without a single word of kindness, the way he's always done. To wash myself off immediately afterwards in the shower. That's no way to put things right.

I called the musician but he wasn't home. As usual, he's off travelling the world, out on the road, who knows where, and he's no good anyway – he's too perfect. Every move he makes is harmonious and elegant. More than anything I love him like a brother.

So I called another one. One of the recent ones.

He's left now. We drank gin and tonics until we were smashed, and then we stumbled into bed. His body slid through my hands like soap, smooth and neutral, not a single vibration of pleasure. We hadn't even finished before he fell asleep like a rock, turning on to his back while I was in the bathroom. I woke him up and kicked him out without saying a word. I put his trousers, underwear and boots into his arms so that he would get dressed outside.

Now I'm here, sitting in front of the open porch door. The perfume of the night is strong, and you can hear the song of the crickets and frogs. I'm sitting here, smoking one cigarette after the other and thinking.

I'd like to close my body up. I'd like my vagina to heal over. I'd like to be able to stop this, stop desiring things that I repent afterwards.

I don't remember a thing about any of the bodies I've touched, that I touch.

I have a protective oily patina coating my skin. It's made out of sperm, sweat and words.

It's obscene.

Fifth Night

It wasn't hard. I used a long, thin, flexible needle. I disinfected it with alcohol and then burned the tip with my lighter. I used an especially robust but thin thread. I didn't use a mirror; I didn't want to watch. I was calm. I sat down on the ground and spread my legs. All I had to do was hold the two edges of flesh together with three fingers. I pushed the needle through with my other hand. I moved slowly, feeling all my muscles tense up, go crazy with pain, and then the needle slide through to the other side. I felt its point against my thumb, and I extracted it. Blood fell to the floor, not much, just a few drops of very pale red.

I kept going to the end, the whole length. Then I cut the thread and tied the two ends together. Done. There was a lot of blood. I felt it slide down me and I listened to the pain throb through my body.

The sky had gone dark outside. It was black, starless, there was just a halo around the moon that I could see through the upper left-hand corner of the window.

I fell asleep, I think, and when I woke, there was pain everywhere. Starting there, and running down my thighs and up to my heart. I disinfected myself with a cotton swab and stretched out on the bed. I swallowed three milligrams of Lorazapam and fell into a glutinous, black, deep sleep.

In my sleep I saw my body. Curled up, inert, lying on the seashore, with cold, black waves washing over it. The very same body I've been using for years as if it didn't belong to me. I have pushed it, flexing the muscles and nerves, into positions that exhausted it. I have made it tremble with shame the way I've forced it to undress

in front of all those different sets of eyes. I have let them abuse it
and I liked that sometimes. I almost always liked it. I've
disrespected my body. I've muffled it with pain.

I'm the one who did it. Not them.

There it is, there, covered with a drape, all curvy lines, hips, bent
knees, arms wrapped around the chest against the cold – or to
protect that fragile zone of the body – the nape of the neck, hair
floating around the throat in a cold-water embrace.

It's a watercolour by Max Klinger, and it was my body. It was
me. *Tossed out on shores of the sea*.

Sixth Night

I was sitting at the kitchen table. He walked around me, agitated. I
could see the beads of sweat on his forehead: a shiny crown of
liquid. His hands were in his pockets.

I told him to come closer. I smelled his young and subtle smell,
soap, no perfume. I saw his gaze, sweet, imploring. I was drowning
in fear. Why him? Why? He's trusting. Perhaps that's why.
Someone who has already been hurt doesn't feel pain so acutely.

I hear his heart beating in the quiet room. I see his fear, the
tension in his muscles.

It lasted a moment. Eyes closed, he held me to him, and when I
felt his erection pressing against me it all turned into the usual
mixed-up, edgeless image.

He'd already become everyone else.

I put my mouth on his, then pressed my head into the hollow of his
shoulder. I reached my arms behind his back and slid down. I put
my hands on the first curve of his bottom, level with his kidneys. I
grasped my left wrist with my right hand and, using this embrace
as leverage, I gathered all my strength and pulled him into me. He
screamed. He didn't stop screaming. I clenched my teeth. Two fat
tears collected in my eyes but didn't drop; they clouded my vision.
When I pushed him away, I averted my eyes. I didn't see anything

but a confusion: his sex was live red flesh, blood falling to the ground, and he kept screaming.

The wind blew strong outside and the branches of the apricot tree, heavy with pinkish-white flowers, rustled in the garden. The stars were luminous. There wasn't a cloud in the sky, not even a shadow darkening that slice of the infinite that covered my house. Finally clear. One lovely night, like when I was child, with the perfume of the honeysuckle and the croaking of the frogs.

He sat on the ground in the corner of the room, his head wedged between the refrigerator and the wall. I could hear him wail. His hands were cupped around his crotch and there was blood on his open trousers, and on his hands, and on the blue tiles. I helped him stand up.

What happened? What happened? I don't understand.

His voice was thick and his eyes were cracked with red veins. I called an ambulance and pushed him out of the door. He didn't understand what was happening and he could barely stand up.

I watched them help him into the back of the ambulance from the window. He kept his head down, like a mule, and he wasn't saying anything.

The branches of the apricot tree seemed to bend even closer, and so did the stars. Such a quiet night, I thought. Now things are in place. Everything is in place.

The moon was high.

Letter to Silence

A face that looks like all the other forgotten faces.

Paul Eluard, 'Belle et resemblante'

As I write this letter, the sky seems made out of cardboard. The outlines of the houses look like a child's cut-outs: neat and even. The way houses are supposed to look but never do.

But today they do. Today I'm starting this letter and everything seems to be in its proper place. The chimneys, the TV aerials, the satellite dishes, the tree branches. Today the light is right and there's barely a sound coming through the closed windows. It's a serene autumn day.

I'm writing this letter in the hope that I'll be able to tell you things. In the hope that some of that blue and green order I see through my window will come into my sentences and make them comprehensible; letters are so intimate it's not always easy to know what they're really about.

I'd like to write you a long letter that will keep you company for many days. A letter to open and close like a music box; whose music keeps playing for a long time – and always sounds different.

Into my letter I'll put all the days and nights we spent together, all the places we went to, and what I felt. As if I were talking to you but not saying anything in particular. I'm not worried about losing you.

I want to remember. And I want you to come so far into my memories that they become yours too. So you can wrap them around you and warm yourself by their fire.

This is how it happened: mouth open and mute. Open over your sex. Open over your lips. Water dripping from your tongue to my mouth. Water dripping from my mouth on to your skin. Droplets that spread into puddles in the shape of clouds. Disappearing in the tiny wrinkles. Dry now. The light in the room was brilliant. It heightened the intensity of the shadows. You didn't say anything.

Not one word. I am silent. As if in prayer, although inside me the words wage a battle, they become confused, they clash. This afternoon, on the dot of three, I looked up at the sky. Your plane was there. It was there for a few moments then disappeared into the pale blue. Leaving just blue behind. All that's left are the unsaid words – a solid, noisy mass in the sky above me. Everything I never told you and that you never told me. A weight like a boulder that I carry on my back.

I look out of the window and see blue and white lines beyond the glass. I only remember frames, fragments of dreams, like film trailers or scraps of old super-eights randomly glued together. When we're alone, our thoughts are free to attack us, to force us to think them even if we don't want to. They run at us, throw themselves at us, clamber over us.

There's a little twelve-year-old boy standing before me. He has blond hair and blue eyes like you. He's a little twelve-year-old boy but the slightest facial movement changes his age. He becomes an adult, or a baby.

I can see every age on your face. I can imagine you as a child, or as a newborn. It's funny: I've seen you covered with talcum powder; I've heard you cry with so much ferocity your tiny face turns red.

In the arms of a woman who isn't me.

I've never before been able to imagine a man as a baby.

I had a dream after the first night. I was climbing these stairs up to a little house in the forest. It was a kind of fort. You were there too, lying on a bed. You'd lost an arm and you were married. Time had passed. What happened? I asked. Life has passed us by, you answered. But I'm still your man.

As I write I see a stone angel, with open, empty eyes and a raised hand. The little boy reaches up to touch the angel. Then the boy dresses up in front of a mirror in an empty house. I'm in the mirror with him. I watch his transformation. Every image makes my heart beat faster.

That's how you made me cry for the first time.

Then smile.

My computer screen is white in the fading afternoon.

Your tongue and lips make invisible tattoos on my face.

Where can I find you?

The scent of your skin around me.

Where can I find you tonight?

Today, when I was eating breakfast, I felt a tickle – a thin strand of blond hair slid down my neck. You had left it behind, twisted into my dark hair.

I can find you in the silence; touching and caressing all the traces you left on me. Silent, like I was then. Silent and praying. I don't know what for. I remember your face, your age-shifting eyes.

Where can I find your hands, your exploring fingers that search the secret geometry of my sex?

Where?

I have to close my eyes and let it all drift away. I have to close my eyes to come in your mouth.

I feel different every time.

I mean, every time I'm with someone new.

Every time I touch someone I feel as if I lose something. I leave parts of me behind. Pieces. Scraps. Like souvenirs that get thrown out after the initial enthusiasm has faded. A doll dressed like a gypsy. A pair of castanets. A glass ball with snow inside.

There's this room, with a bed. A big bed that takes up almost all the space. A window. The dawn light takes no pity on our bodies, our tired eyes, on my fear.

The sheets are clean. I imagine the hotel maid sending them flying out over the mattress with a fresh, breezy flick in the morning when she makes the bed. The sea air coming in through the window.

You slept for a week on this bed. Before I came along.

While you were in the shower, I nosed through your things. The box of condoms was black and red. There were four left. I read on the outside of the box: *Ten pieces*. Japanese condoms, in shiny black plastic packets with red writing on them. I imagined the rooms, the women, the time of day or night, the clean sheets in other hotel rooms. When? When was the last time?

Silence. To write without words. Perhaps it depends on the syntax – on arranging the words so that they assume different roles, they hit with new impact.

Have you ever thought about it? There are very few people with whom you can sit in silence. People think that being together means talking and so words become expressions of panic, embarrassment, used to fill the empty moments. But to be together in silence is rich, it's a way of sharing what's essential. Happiness is inexplicable. It's like a calm water rising in you, moving slowly, following a rhythm like a heartbeat.

With you, I felt something like that.

I've written many letters.

I've written at different times, in different languages. I've bought every type of stamp. I've written longhand, on the typewriter, on the computer.

This time, I'd like to try to write with silence.

I always try to remember details in order to hold on to something that memory's instantaneous incinerator would otherwise destroy.

The long, deep scar on your arm. The pins and plates that I can feel under the skin.

The letter sketched by a vein on your sex when it's hard. A kind of upside-down P. There's the familiar red scar on the left side of your stomach. A tumour they extracted; it matches the one I have on the left of my spine. A vertical birthmark, like a little grain of rice in the middle of your chest. A strawberry one on the back of your neck. A little puddle of yellow gold in your left eye, like a grain of pyrite.

All these weeks and months spent trying to remember details of bodies that are void of interest. Bodies made of muscle and bone, the smell of skin, sweat, sperm, hair. Bodies I passed over blindly, with minimal interest – just enough to understand the basic mechanisms.

It was different with you. I tried to learn you by heart.

I learned something about myself. Your hands and lips traced my contours, defined their borders and gave everything a name.

They were names I'd never heard before, pronounced in a language that I don't know well.

They seemed like magic words. Words that should have unleashed my body and transformed it into a forest – a marvellous, unknown place where I could dig myself in and get lost.

Today, my eyes alternate between full and empty. Full and empty like all the open spaces of my body now that you're gone.

I was filled up. By you. My head was consumed by images of you.

And there's a whole universe of words I don't know, that relate to you.

Every contact between skin and skin, between tongue and thought, needs a new translation according to rules I haven't learned yet. I seek them out, the way, in fairy tales, they are always looking for a captured princess. There might be a trail of breadcrumbs that shimmers in the moonlight. A glass slipper or a single hair in the dust. I look for the key that will open the magic casket. It might be a word. Or a silent sigh.

There's a man here I like. I have a picture of him taken in front of the sea – the same sea that was outside our hotel room.

One hand is raised to hold on to his hat, the other is clutching some sheets of paper. He's reading.

He's a very beautiful man, bald, with a perfectly round head. And he has a gentle voice.

Every time he phones me, we remain silent for a while, before the words come.

I'm talking about this man to pass the time. But my eyes alternate between full and empty today. I have before me calm water and a white bed splashed with light. A sheet ripping – an unpleasant sound – between my arm and yours.

I was talking about that man in the picture. Reading by the sea. Bald head, elegant hands. I recognise my own pauses in his conversation. The two of us should have a drink together. I would like that.

I don't know why I'm talking about him in this letter to you. Maybe because it's just a lovely picture, and there are so many stories in that image. Possibilities engraved in ochre, blue – a blue so much more intense than any real blue – in soft magenta, in a limit of yellow on skin.

When words fail me, I know that another image will come and reawaken them.

We've talked about silence. A silent film. Books with lots of white spaces. But we live in chaos. Often we choose it. It's in the multiplicity of voices and stories, the sounds of the city around us, telephone calls, fax machines, answering machines, in coffee machines with all the noise they make: boiling water running through a filter and into a glass pot with a muted splash – a waterfall in a bubble. Disconnected conversations, music at full blast, the bass thundering through your heart and stomach. Neffa's lyrics follow me everywhere: *I look for new light in the confusion*.

But we didn't bring anything to that white bed. Just the light and our naked bodies. Meaningless words that are silence between lovers. Nothing musical. The squish of my sex opening and closing, wet beneath your fingers, the cracking of joints: sounds from within our bodies. The sheets ripping, skin rubbing against skin or material.

I imagine your white house that I've only seen pictures of, the shadows of green trees all around it. I imagine paper, sheets of paper rustling in your hands. I imagine you sitting inside, in the shade, with the stone angel behind you. A stone angel with empty eyes like the ones at the church of St Merry in Paris.

Mouth open and mute.

Your white teeth. Your pink gums. A pink that comes from multivitamins no cigarettes lots of fruit and vegetables not too much meat limited drug use and plenty of water.

I know there's silence there when you work, between the trees. I know that you don't speak to anyone for days at a time.

I read a book by Geoff Dyer called *The Search*. The cover calls it 'A Metaphysical Noir'. It's about a man following another man around an enormous country that might be the United States – though it doesn't say – and he goes from one city to another and they all have names that correspond to their essence. It's a little like Calvino's *Invisible Cities*. In one city the man finds a cassette recorder with a tape inside. He pushes *play* and silence comes out. It's not simply *nothing*. It's not *silence*. It's *a* silence. The specific silence of a city, or a room, of a certain hour of the day or night. The man buys a lot of tapes before he sets off again, and in each one of the cities, in every hotel room, he turns the cassette recorder on and captures the moment and the spirit of the place: its silence.

I keep on writing. The afternoon is made of rubber. It melts away under the sun's last rays. It sticks to the roofs of houses, to the branches of trees, to everything. It's blue and orange and darkens quickly.

There's a desert in your words sometimes that I can't cross. You say that you're peaceful in a voice belonging to someone who has stopped asking questions. You're tired. But when I met you you were vital, reckless, impassioned, lyrical, devastating, devastated, a bastard, and alive. I wanted you like that even if perhaps it wasn't you. Now that you're far away, unreachable, totally in another life, I keep thinking that you're everyone I ever wanted, exactly what I want – in spite of everything. The bitterness lingers, because you're bitter. But your body sings: not of tenderness, only of the body. I love you like the first day, the way I love the house where I lived when I was little, the way I love my mother, the way I love the wind.

Your sex in my mouth and your clasped hands massaging the back of my neck.

The first time you kissed me we were sitting at a bar. There was Cuban music playing and someone talking loudly nearby. I was drunk on gin and tonics, my head was spinning. It was very hot – it was June after all.

The kisses came like words. They had the same restless shape. The words came first. I watched your mouth and saw them: bright, cold crystals. They beat a dirt track through the wildflowers. Dry and rugged. Your words echoed in the night, building a house without windows or doors.

Will you ever come back?

To this house, to these empty rooms?

I don't know. I keep writing letters in order to accumulate sentences. It's a burden, you know.

They confuse me.

The light breaks over the table; the tea in my cup is steaming near my arm. I spend entire afternoons with my hand clutching a pen or my fingers beating uncertainly on the keyboard. All around me are sheets of paper covered with notes, notes copied on to the cold screen to make them real.

And memories. Memories like awaited dinner guests who arrive and knock on the door before revealing themselves.

Memories.

Do you remember the first time we met? We were in the foyer of a cinema and you smiled at me. I saw your black-and-white snake-skin cowboy boots and wanted to laugh. Leather trousers and long blond Swedish hair. Too flashy. Too many perfect teeth, neon-blue eyes and the complexion of a vegetarian. I turned away, and laughed. But you kept staring at me. You laughed at my motorcycle boots. A puss in boots, you said to me later, who seemed to come from a weird fairy tale.

These uncertain lines, wobbling like ants overwhelmed by the burden on their backs, have no purpose. I know that.

A girl sits in an empty room writing a love letter to someone far away.

I dislike being so banal. But perhaps love is always like this. It might even be the redundancy and banality of its expression that makes it so sacred and unique, and constantly new.

Little reflections. The light falls around the house. The field outside my window fills with muted shivers. Cats, hares, striped snails, racing dogs. I watch it. I'm never alone. I have the country-side and I have paper at my fingertips. I have the soft rhythmic tapping on the dirty white computer keyboard.

On the platform at the train station I saw a man walking fast. A cloud had got caught on his hat and seemed to be following him. He was carrying an overnight bag. Who knows where he was going in such a hurry. That was the cold afternoon when you told me you loved me. You called me Paola, but I knew you were talking to me. Time had passed since the first time.

You were tired. Your eyes were bright and your nails were bitten down to the skin.

The man and his cloud had disappeared. I took your hand without saying anything. The right words always come to me too late. Sometimes, they take years to come.

Excuse me for now, I have to stop writing. It's cold and I need to get something to eat.

In this house, the rough transparent curtains shift in the breeze and deaden all colour. The shadows are like sighs. I imagine there is an ocean beyond the window. Just like in that room where we stayed so many years ago. White, vaporous curtains and the sea outside. The smooth shimmering sea under the June sun. You told me about nimble ships skimming the waters, carrying men and their dreams. We watched the constellations light up like street lamps as soon as the sun sank below the horizon. I've never seen stars like that over my foggy plains. We drank a lot. And the sea was always there, even if it was constantly changing colours.

I ran my fingers through your dark hair. Soft, compact waves. I slid my palms over your sunburned skin, and it was smooth like a mirror made out of water. Your eyes would suddenly flash. The night didn't scare me then as it does now. It was summer.

Summer is always less frightening. It's autumn now, and that means spending more time at home alone. I watch the comet shower through the window and my lips leave round, white haloes on the glass – invisible from the outside.

Periodically I get up but I come back. The computer screen is still glowing though the room is dark now. The way the letters tremble hurts my eyes. The sheets of paper covered in drafts of my letters are like old rags, the edges worn down from the way I finger them – a tic I've had since primary school.

You never noticed.

Maybe because you were even more restless than me. Sitting quietly at the desk next to mine, the professors' voices floating over our heads without touching them. Your hands twisting a paper tissue. Your knuckles were white. Hands clenched around the paper. Teeth clenched. You'd clench your eyes shut sometimes when the light came in too brightly through the windows. Those winters spent in the grey-walled room weren't happy. We'd hide real literature on our laps under the desk and read it in secret. Notebooks and textbooks on top: in meticulous order. The pens in a row. But they were never our pens and we'd always leave them behind.

Sometimes you wore make-up to school. Black eyeliner, mascara, lipstick. Your hair seemed lighter when you were wearing make-up and I wanted to touch you. I'd go into a cubicle in the toilets to read your notes, coffee or a cigarette in the other hand. I spent a lot of time like that. I'd miss lessons but that never bothered me. There was the sky outside, there were many possible futures, our life there on the inside was like a science-fiction movie on pause. Then one day, over Christmas, we were walking in the rain. The city wasn't new any more. It seemed to belong to another century. I'd try to focus my thoughts by imagining the clopping of horses' hoofs and the swish of carriages. We walked arm in arm. The rain fell on us. We laughed about nothing. All we had was urgency.

The same urgency that's making me run all over the house to close the shutters. A cold wind has lifted and is beating against the walls and the trees. It is starting to rain. Like water tipped from a bucket. It won't last long.

I'm leaving this letter. But I'll come back.

I'll come back.

The first time we met was in September in the corridor at school. You were wearing a pale cotton jumper. The first thing I noticed were your breasts, then your eyes. They were cat's eyes. They probably still are. Yellow.

The rain has stopped. The bucket is empty. There's the smell of rain everywhere, even inside. Even with the windows closed. The gutters are draining and the wind is blowing through the trees, blowing them dry. I press a key, and start a new page. I leave space between one line and the next. I want to give air to the thoughts. I breathe.

The first time I embraced you I wasn't sure you wanted me to. It was summer. The wind blew against us. Your motorbike purred and you smiled. Your shirt was pink, like the distant horizon over the fields outside my window. A fragile pink, that dissolved quickly.

The second time I felt blue fabric beneath my fingers. And your strong muscles. The wild smell of your skin. The scent of sage and a faint trace of lemon on your lips. I kissed the corners of your mouth wet with rain. I waited.

The rain followed us from the beginning.

I put my lips on yours and you said, Are you sure I'm the one you really want? You know that there's never been anyone else and how badly you can hurt me. But I wasn't listening. I looked out of the car window at the November sky. There was no fog that evening. Your hair was still long. And you were already a little scared of me. How many nights had we spent looking out at the still stars over the icy fields, hands buried in our pockets, the music blaring on the car radio. Gin and tonic in paper cups, and words. There seemed to be too many words then, but remembering them now, they seem too few. They have evaporated like alcohol. You spoke of platforms in the middle of the sea, starry nights alone, the cold. Of faraway places. After all, who was making you stay here in the plains? But you stay.

I stay too, even though I could also leave. I stay here with you.

And the words that I write with these cold hands as this night falls are for you, they're all for you.

The first time that you came off the train, your arms were full of books. And like all the other times that followed, you smiled, and that made you seem older and I loved you even more.

It's a strange thing: the love is even more intense now that it's over and become harmless and sweet with time. I remember everything clearly – but hold no grudges.

Does that make my memories less true?

And when you hugged me I could feel the edges of the books in your bag and smell your perfume. I imagined the parallel hug – the converse of ours, the hug you gave the woman you left to come to me.

The night sinks into black. I can't see anything through the glass. The street lamps have gone off. We're into the second half of the night: it's more sullen. It scares me. Now the memories crystallise. Now my hands get tired and so do my sentences. My letter becomes old suddenly, hollow, barely a frightened whisper. I revive days, nights, places and things. I feel like a sorcerer's apprentice, a little wizard trying to combine voices and times, even though it might be dangerous. Refusing to give in to fear or sleep.

I want to tell you everything. I want to think everything and write everything. I want to tell you everything I haven't told you. To make a noise, and prolong that distended and distorted noise, keep twisting it until it makes music.

I want to tell you everything.

Your face, your hands, your voice and the things you left behind accumulate around me. They dress me. The clothes change according to the season and fashion; your fragile gifts turn into regal clothes worn by princesses in fairy tales, or into the threadbare rags of a beggar.

Words don't reach the hot centre. Words flake under your grip; they're brittle fingernails to be filed or buffed.

There's not enough time. The night is almost over and sleep wants me. If I were able, the way I was as a child, to make the silence sing I would close my eyes now, lift my fingers – just slightly – into the air and make things dance.

If I were still able.

The minimal architecture of this letter is dissolving. Can't you tell?
It's falling to pieces, becoming entangled. Maybe written words, like events and people, gather around a nucleus in a configuration that it is impossible to plot.

There's silence in my room. The kind of silence that you only hear at night. The leaves of the birch tree rustle like coins someone is jangling in their closed fist.
I have been writing all day and all night. This letter has taken time. The world seems to have disappeared. There's no one in the house.
I'm here and I feel the distance.

I found your note in my diary. A little piece of paper, with spidery pencil marks on it. Then I found the others. All written in pen, with coloured ink, or black. And then more. Written with gestures that can't be read from paper. I'm the only one who remembers those gestures.
Thank you.
For the sadness you planted in me. So much time had passed since anyone had touched me so deeply.
I feel like I'm dissolving.

In silence.

A concentrated, fluid silence. Like water that flows over the skin, knowingly following its curves.

That specific silence that is exactly like love.

Fugue

. . . this is the silent road through
the hawthorn hedge, sweet labyrinth
of home, far away, so far
around one bend and it disappears

where the dust pretends a vagabond
child and the day's adventure.

Attilio Bertolucci, 'La Polvere'

This is the road I've taken every morning this year. Almost a year, it's March now and school started in September.

I was still in lower school last year, and that building was closer than this one, about a quarter of a mile closer. Sometimes after school I'd find my mother waiting for me in the car, but I explained to her that now I'm in the upper school I'm old enough to carry my own rucksack.

It takes ten minutes to walk from my house to school: 10,100 steps, forty trees, two rose bushes, thirty-two houses and a park, lots of pillar boxes, lots and lots of lampposts, loads of parked cars and a church.

And a little girl in a window, standing behind the glass.

When it's hot, or if I'm in a hurry, I take my bike, otherwise I walk. It's still the same road, but everything changes depending on your means of transport. She's just a flash when I'm on my bike. I turn my head to look at her in the window and risk crashing into a parked car or a tree.

She's little. Really just a baby.

One day when I was walking past, I waved hello. The curtains were pulled back and she was sitting on her yellow chair – that looked way too small for her already. She raised her tiny hand to wave back at me; her fingers stiff and spread like a fan. She opened her mouth and moved her lips, but since I had my Walkman on, I couldn't hear anything.

I don't like little kids. Very little ones, I mean, the ones who haven't started school yet, the ones who whine constantly and are always saying, Buy this for me? Buy this for me? And they pick their noses and scratch themselves. You look at them cross-eyed and they start to cry.

But the little girl in the window was different.

She is different.

She'd grown since the very first time I saw her. Babies change in just a few months. And she'd changed too.

My mother says that I've always been a bully, even when I was in nursery school. I don't remember it that well, but I think maybe she's right. I was just trying to have fun, to make friends. Or defend myself. Maybe I did it to prove that I existed. Whatever, I'm sure I was trying to make friends, even if I went about it the wrong way – angrily. That's the way I've always done things: the wrong way with the right intentions.

Little kids don't understand about friendship. All they ever hear is teachers and grown-ups complaining. Not all little kids though. The little girl in her plastic chair was different.

Skin was playing on my Walkman the first time I waved. It was a foggy white morning, and there was the good smell of real autumn in the air; it was already almost winter.

Skin's voice wailing in my ear, I'm pedalling happily, pushing hard, standing up off the seat, cycling against the wind.

Before going to sleep the night before, I'd watched the moon from our terrace. The sky was velvet dark and there were stars everywhere. I do that every night. I stand there and think. I didn't care how cold it was or that my fingers were frozen. I stood there in silence, looking at the night, smelling, greeting it with my muscles. The street lights were almost all out, so it was really dark. After a while the stars and the moon illuminated the black sky as if it were day: a strange day made out of shadows, but if you looked hard, you could still see things.

After I turned fourteen everything got brighter, more important. I can feel things inside pulling me in different directions. I can feel myself growing, getting big and tall. So what if I'm still only five feet tall? My body doesn't feel like it can contain me. It's as if the tips of my fingers and toes extend for thousands of miles, spooky tendrils poking through my skin and running wild trying to touch everything, to know everything, to live more quickly. *More*. It's a great feeling that's scary, too, sometimes. It's scary because I might not ever be able to live more. Perhaps no one can and everyone has feelings like this at some time in their life, but nothing changes and they live the same old life and don't tell anyone that there were times when they could touch the stars.

The little girl waved at me every morning from her chair. And she didn't always stay sitting; sometimes she'd get up to stand by the window in her coloured pyjamas and wait for me. She waved woodenly and I could see her lips move but couldn't hear what she was saying, and I didn't want to either. I liked seeing her mouth open and her fingers reach out as if they were trying to touch me, while I listened to the distorted guitar in Soundgarden's 'The Fourth of July'. The fourth of July is my birthday. I don't understand the lyrics, because they're in English, but I get the title. It's better that way, I can imagine they're singing right to me.

If they'd let me, I'd listen to music in school too. The teachers' voices are like chainsaws cutting into my brain, which is a shame, because school could be great – I think. I mean, it could be great to go to school, to sit at my desk by the window and have a conversation with someone who cares about what I have to say. But teachers just talk to hear the sound of their own voices. They read aloud or explain something; it doesn't matter if you don't get it. No one ever listens to them. Well, there are maybe three or four people in my class who are obsessed with studying and getting good marks. They're the ones who desperately check their Latin homework ten minutes before lessons start. They hunch over their desks like moles, with their glasses and cool, self-satisfied expressions, because they studied until ten and then went to sleep thinking about the test. Everyone else is faking it. Everyone else copies the homework and gets to school late, headphones jammed into their ears and a lost expression on their faces.

I'm reading a Stephen King book, *The Dark Half*. I like the part about the birds. A dense cloud of black birds crying through the blue sky. That phrase gets repeated over and over every couple of pages. They're the same birds I see in the park every morning on the way to school. A tight black flock, so closely packed they look like a moving inkstain. It's like they've gone crazy for the blue sky and the sun. They fly in a circle, as if they need to be together, each one with its beak tucked into the tail of the next. As they whirl round they hardly change position and they cast a big black shadow over the field.

I don't know why I took her. They're calling it *kidnapping*. But I just took her. I had every intention of giving her back. Like a bicycle that you take because you're in a hurry to get somewhere, then you bring it back to where you found it, and that's the end of it. If you're lucky the owner doesn't even notice it was gone.

They blew the whole thing out of proportion. As far as I was concerned, it was much simpler. Clean. Like a short, perfect note.

The sky when all the clouds suddenly disappear, a violent blue, swept clean by a gust of wind from far away.

I took her. She was there, waiting for me, like she had been every morning. She was wearing her yellow pyjamas, the ones with the pictures of hot-air balloons on them. Her hair was unbrushed and full of knots, there was still sleep in her eyes, as if she'd just woken up and hadn't even had breakfast yet. When she saw me, she lifted her arm, and I suddenly realised there was no glass between us. The window was open and she was on the windowsill, barefoot.

I dropped my bike on the grass. I climbed over the low garden fence. She was watching me, her eyes calm, unafraid. She knew who I was; I was her morning friend. There was no sound from inside the house; it seemed empty. I took her in my arms and she didn't say anything. She reached her arms up around my neck and she smelled of Nivea and talcum powder. I climbed back over the fence, straining my legs and using my free arm to pull us over. She was hanging on to me like a creeping vine. On the other side, I lost my balance and we fell, but we didn't get hurt. The headphones of my Walkman were all tangled up inside the hood of my sweatshirt and the cord was strangling me. I unwound it and put the headphones to her ears, pressing the play button through the pocket of my jeans and 'Until It Sleeps' started up. The tape had got to the beginning of the song at exactly the moment I had seen her standing in the window. She laughed. Metallica isn't exactly music for babies, but she was a different kind of baby.

Different.

I wasn't thinking about anything in particular as I placed her on the bar of my black and yellow bike. I held my arms protectively around her, two powerful barriers to keep her from sliding to the ground. I pedalled and pedalled. Fast, but not too fast. There weren't many people out. No one we passed even looked at us, I was going too fast and the little girl was hidden behind the sleeves of my jacket. Tiny thing.

I headed out into the countryside, along a dirt road. The gravel flew up from under my bicycle wheels. I left a crooked track in the stones and dust behind me.

I got to the Villa dei Sospiri. It's one of my favourite places. I've always liked it, ever since I was little. I've always imagined that I'd bring my first girlfriend here, on some summer night with a full moon and bright stars. The perfume of the fields and the song of the crickets around us.

The Villa dei Sospiri is an old house in ruins. There are plants growing inside, not just moss, but grass and flowers, even full-size trees, tall and strong after all these years. A long time has passed since the bomb fell here.

There's a story about this house that has to do with its name. My father told it to me, something romantic and useless, the kind of story that girls and old men like.

I've forgotten it, the way I forget everything I don't care about. I don't like stories. Any stories. I don't even like films. I like things that happen and then are over and disappear without a trace. I don't want to be thinking about motives or consequences. It's over and that's that.

There was no one around. The fields were silent and still pale from the light frost that forms in March. I unloaded her by the edge of the ditch, tossed the bike over to the other side, and then helped her across. Nettles stung her bare feet and they started swelling up with blisters. She began to cry, but didn't make any noise. Tears rolled down her face and I didn't know what to do. I led her into the house. There was no roof, so you could look right through to the open sky, except in one place where the second floor was still intact. The tree branches grew so close together that it was quite dark inside. I made her sit on one of the bottom steps of the staircase and blew on her feet to make the burning go away, but she had already stopped crying.

I spread my jacket on the ground and made her lie on it. She was really small now that I could look at her properly, close up. I covered her legs with the edge of the jacket.

Go to sleep, I told her. I'm going away for a minute, but I'll be right back with some food. You have to promise not to move, or scream. You have to be quiet here. Go to sleep. I'll be right back.

She looked up at me with the calmest eyes in the world, as if she either didn't understand what I was saying or understood so completely that she had gone beyond my words, beyond my thoughts, even deeper – into the thoughts I hadn't even thought yet. She was calm and all red in the face, like she had sunburn. Her eyes were bright, empty.

I didn't worry about her on my way back into town. I knew she was safe and wouldn't move – although there was no reason for me to be so sure, other than the fact that what I'd seen in her eyes made me think of an alien. She was like a monster from outer space, super-intelligent and neutral – emotionless. Sitting there in an abandoned house, but not questioning it, as if she were at home in her garden.

On the run again. I had to be careful not to get caught. At that point, I was already half an hour late for school. I could imagine all my classmates sitting in their usual places, packed into dwarf-sized wooden desks, with their vacuous expressions. Bertolani, the kid who shares my desk, would have all his peppermints lined up in an orderly row behind his pile of books and pens.

I went the long way round to get to the supermarket, along the deserted roads that circle the fields.

I suddenly started thinking about all the other mornings I'd spent the same way: a spontaneous decision to cut school and sneak on to the shuttle bus for college students and commuters going into Bologna. The bus stops right in front of my school. I'd check out of the corner of my eye to make sure there were no spies on the bus – a neighbour, or one of my mother's friends – and then I'd move. I'd launch myself through the door into the warmth, the smell of foam rubber from the ripped leather seats, the acrid smell of sweat and perfume. The long road through the fields, the gentle curves that make your breakfast come up into your mouth. I couldn't just hang out in the village. It's too small and there aren't any coffee shops where you can sit for the whole morning waiting for school to finish and your mates to come through the school doors. I always went into the city, where I'd sit in a coffee shop until ten thirty, then go to play video games. By myself.

I thought about other mornings just like this one, but damper, with dim lights and sad skies. Wasted mornings, waiting. The computerised sounds of intergalactic warfare, Formula One racing cars and defeated warriors. The juke box in the background. Other people's cigarettes filling the room with a dense fog, the stink of bodies and plastic, the stench of car-exhaust fumes drifting in through the open door, accompanied by an endless stream of clones with matching rucksacks and eyes already glazed over from the first joint of the day.

Long, nauseating mornings, filled with a growing sense of guilt: the sense that you were dropping things along the road but didn't even know what you'd lost.

I was wasting time now too. But she was there, and that was reason enough. This creature who was so different from me. To study. To learn about.

At the supermarket, I bought apricot juice, biscuits, two sandwiches, a piece of pizza and two unripe bananas.

I shivered when I got back to the Villa. I suddenly started wondering what would happen if she had wandered off, or if someone had found her and asked her why she was there, who had brought her. That someone might still be there, lying in wait to catch me, to fuck me over. Crouched silently in the corner, motionless, one hand over the little girl's mouth to keep her from crying. Trying to screw me over.

But there wasn't anyone there. I pulled aside the low branches to get to the corner where I'd left her.

She was sitting cross-legged on my jacket, looking at me, an incomprehensible and peaceful expression on her flat almost oriental little face. Her eyes were grey and cold like two stones.

That gaze scared me. I don't know why.

I moved towards her cautiously. Stepping carefully on the dry leaves so I wouldn't make any noise. Stupid, I know. But I couldn't bear the idea of scaring her, of doing anything that would make her expression change.

I put the bag with the stuff I'd bought down in front of her and sat, too, legs crossed.

She just kept looking at me. Her hands on her knees, her fists balled up. She looked me right in the eyes and didn't blink. Her pupils were stony and dry, not a shadow. Hard, transparent eyes.

I asked her if she wanted something to eat. She didn't answer, but reached out for the bag and dug into it. I watched her tear at a piece of bread, bringing it to her mouth and cramming it in, her palms open, like a wild girl.

Some wind was coming in. You could feel a kind of whistle blowing through what had once been rooms, running through the house and then disappearing somewhere out into the trees, into the cluster of leaves.

I was cold without my jacket, but didn't have the heart to take it away from her. She had wrapped it around herself. She looked like a puffball, with just her head and hands sticking out.

She suddenly spoke to me. Her mouth full of sandwich and her greasy hand pointing at herself.

My name is Giulia, what's yours?

It was the first thing I'd heard her say. I answered.

I'm Cris.

Our conversation was over. She didn't say another word, but started staring at me again. Maybe she was waiting for me to say something. Or maybe, everything that we had to say to each other had already been said. Giulia and Cris. Giulia and Cris are hidden in an abandoned house one sunny, windy March morning.

Something moved in the hedges and scared me. I jumped up and looked over my shoulder. My heart was beating wildly like it was going to burst out through my shirt. It wasn't anything, maybe a cat, or a lizard. Maybe a blackbird. Nothing. But now I was frightened. It was like I'd suddenly woken up from a dream. What was I doing here with a baby girl? Why had I brought her here? Something had taken me over. If I had really wanted to escape, I could have come here alone. I could have come with Bertolani to chill out and smoke a couple of joints. Even better, I could have brought a girl.

She stayed there, still and quiet.

When I sat back down, she reached up to my face, leaning over towards me. She touched my mouth with her pizza-greasy finger.

I calmed down. This was a kind of excursion. A day of wind and blue sky. And she was my morning friend. I'd had the courage to take her. Because I wanted to. This was a test, if I could take her, I could do whatever else I wanted to. For ever.

I lifted my shirt to scratch my stomach. My hand slid over my dry skin, feeling my muscles contract suddenly, a spasm, or maybe it was the cold and the nausea. Her eyes locked on the strip of skin between the belt of my jeans and my shirt.

I really don't know. I don't know why I did it, but that was how it started. I took her hand and placed it there, in that exact place.

Feel my muscles, I told her. These are my abdominal muscles, do you feel them? Her hand was soft and her eyes were still peaceful.

What am I doing? I thought. What the hell am I doing?

I was scared, and felt ridiculous. But I wanted her to keep her hand on my skin. I liked it. I touched her too, I stroked her like a kitten. Her soft belly, her neck, her armpits. Her skin was smooth and so transparent I could see all the little blue veins. She let me touch her.

Not like Lisa. Every time I tried to get up Lisa's shirt, she'd pull it down and say, No, come on. Not now. It was always, *Not now*. She just wanted to kiss me, with her tongue and everything, but that was all.

Lisa had tits and when she wore a tank top you could see a tuft of brown soft hair under her arms. But the little girl was flat and smooth. A living doll, unmarred.

When I moved her hands down to the fly of my jeans, she didn't resist.

I unzipped them and her hand moved, her eyes became curious. She squeezed her fingers around my sex, she hurt me a little. But it was good too. It was the first time that any hand other than my own had touched me there.

The first time.

I didn't look at her, I watched the sky. Through the blanket of dark leaves and the hole in the wall, I could see the fields brightening with sun.

Suddenly I felt a rip, as if someone were pulling my insides out with a string, and the string had become all tangled up in my guts. I closed my eyes for a second. I didn't see anything, just a confusion of red spots, like when you've looked too long at the sun and then you go into the dark and you can't see anything around you because your pupils are still burning from the light.

She smiled.

I touched her. Her pyjamas were fastened between her legs with poppers. I ran my finger over the metal studs, and she lowered her eyelids.

Enough. Time to stop. I got to my feet, did up my trousers. I felt sick, the nausea was turning in my stomach. I leaned against the wall and spewed my guts out over the leaves of a bush. I felt so stupid and ridiculous. And still, the little girl didn't cry, she sat there calmly. I was disgusting. If only she would start screaming, or try to stop me. A final heave of vomit, my hand resting on the cold wet stone of the old house.

What a weird morning. They were probably already looking for her. Her mother must be scared to death. Maybe she was crying. I could imagine her: I saw her in her pyjamas and dressing gown, with her hair all messed up and her face wet with tears, her cold, pale hands clutched together.

I didn't know what to do. She was still there, her hands back in the shopping bag, tearing at the greasy pizza wrapper. She was so small, just like a porcelain doll. Her pretty eyes were calm, her cheeks red from the icy wind. She was probably going to get ill. What an arsehole. Arsehole.

I'm going to leave now, I thought. I'll leave her here, someone will find her – that's what I thought as I watched her.

Then I heard a noise. There was sound of brakes on gravel down on the road in front of the house. A car. I remembered I'd left my bike by the side of the ditch. You couldn't miss it. I heard the metallic click and slam of car doors opening and closing. Three identical sounds. Three doors.

I went over to look through a crack in the wall. And there were three of them. Two uniformed policemen, guns and all, and an older man dressed in black, like a priest, but it wasn't a priest. I didn't know who it was, I'd never seen him before.

They were looking up at the house. One of them had pulled the bike up off the grass and was holding it by the handlebars, examining it like he'd never seen a bike before.

I had to get out of there. I had to escape. Fast. I looked around. The far side of the house was even more ruined. There was a gaping hole where there must have once been a door. Branches and leaves covered the opening that led out to the fields. I went through it and the bright sunlight almost knocked me over. The field was a gigantic lake of thick grass waving in the wind. Dark, wet green. I plunged into it. I ran with all the strength I had in my legs and lungs. I ran, knowing it was useless. They were going to find the little girl, and they had my bike.

Suddenly, I stopped wanting to escape. I threw myself forward as if I were diving into a real lake of warm, soothing water. I slid face down into the grass. It was cool and smelled rich. I could feel the solid ground under my stomach. I closed my eyes; I listened to the wind. I thought I might fall asleep there. And dream. And touch the clouds with my long arms, my new muscles.

The little girl didn't cry, didn't scream, didn't say anything. She let the man in black take her into his arms. That's what my father said. Her mother cried when they brought her back, but the little girl didn't. She looked up at her mother, dry-eyed and peaceful. The only thing she said was: *Cris*.

The little girl's parents didn't talk to me; they talked about me. They tried to scare me. Then I figured out that no one had pressed charges. In the end, the little girl was fine, nothing serious had happened. I kept my head lowered, and nodded periodically. But inside, I was thinking of the green field, the abandoned house, the sound of the wind, the sun, of the sense of freedom I had had that day. I thought about how my muscles had leaped out towards the blue. I thought about Giulia's steady eyes, how much her eyes looked like little grey stones.

I still take the same road. Sometimes I walk, more often I cycle. Sometimes, Giulia is standing in the window, wearing her colourful pyjamas. I pass by quickly, turn my head, and she puts her hand on the glass to wave hello. Sometimes, I see only a halo of white condensation in the shape of her little fingers. I walk past quickly and smile into the wind, headphones tight over my ears, and the birds flying black over the park. They move so much faster than I do.

Journey in Red Shoes

But when the sands swallow up the memory,
the throbbing pain is cut short.
That's all.

Elsa Morante, 'Children Saved the World'

Our shoes are prettier than Miou's. Her feet are too small, the shop didn't have any shoes like ours in her size. So she cried.

Our shoes are shiny red-patent leather, shiny like an apple just polished on your dress. They have a thin strap that fastens with a round button – also red. They have round toes and low, white rubber heels.

Miou has red shoes with a strap too, but they have a square toe and an ugly yellow plastic flower instead of a red button.

Miou cried the whole way home. And then she kept crying while we were packing our bags.

Miou cries all the time.

Mummy doesn't pay much attention any more; her ears are as full as ours are by now.

Miou's screams are shrill and relentless, like a siren, or the car horns down on the street. They're harsh, dry screams, without tears. Miou cries dry. Like dark desperation.

We're thirteen years old and Miou is only four. What does she know of dark desperation? In school we read books about war.

But that doesn't have anything to do with it: it's not Miou's fault she's so young.

She's crying again and I try not to hear her. I close my eyes and hold her to me. I brush her hair, and bounce my legs to comfort her.

All you can see out of the window are white clouds being dragged around by an unforgiving blue.

Why must this child make me feel so desperate? Can't Miou see how peacefully her sisters sit, side by side, chattering quietly? Why can't she learn from them? Why?

I'm so tired I could fall asleep at this very moment and sleep a whole lifetime away. When I awoke, Miou would be dead and buried, not even a distant memory. Her cries would be lost in the empty sky. Far away.

But instead she keeps crying, louder and louder, and I want to throw her out. I want to see Miou sucked up into the air and flying off, her little shape getting smaller and smaller as she flies further and further away. And the sound of her crying getting smaller and further away.

Marcella and Giacinta look at their new shoes and talk about things they want. The desires of thirteen-year-olds: an apple-green suede miniskirt, a perm, new roller skates, the latest CD.

I have thirteen-year-old desires too, but I can't talk about them. I want a new outfit with a long, tight skirt, and a set of expensive face creams, Dior or Shiseido, in satiny jars that I can keep in a neat row on the shelf under the bathroom mirror. I want a big bathtub with a Jacuzzi setting and I want a new lover. I want someone to take me in his arms and whisper sweet things in my ear. I want someone to take me to the cinema and on long walks under starry skies.

I want Miou to stop whimpering and sweating on my lap. I want people to stop looking at me and my little girl, who drools, cries and pees herself. I want to be happy too, just like they are. But instead . . .

Miou is still screaming. We can't understand why Mummy doesn't just slap her sometimes and make it all stop. She hugs her tight to her chest and whispers into her ear.

Still Miou won't stop.

Miou will never stop – we know that.

We swing our legs, watching the way the light hits the shiny toes of our four twin shoes. We look out of the window, and flick through one of Mummy's magazines. We're not in any hurry. We're not going to cry, not even when the plane takes off. Even though we know that we'll never set foot here again. Never again. We vowed. Never again.

I'll never come back to this country. I know it, I can feel it. When the plane takes off, that'll be the last time I look down on Athens: the white and grey jumble of houses with their windows like thousand of eyes. The polluted green port of Piraeus.

I'll shut my eyes and wait until I'm far away, very far away.

Miou has climbed down from Mummy's lap and she's walking up and down the blue-carpeted aisle. She rests her hands on the backs of people's chairs; she grabs their arms. Everyone pretends it's nothing, they smile, because she's so little, and it seems cruel to be annoyed by weeping babies. They think maybe she's scared of planes, and that she'll stop soon.

But she won't stop; we know it.

One day Miou started crying and she hasn't stopped since.

We don't mind leaving Athens. We had an ugly house. There was noise everywhere – in the street, in the house. We got used to it, but we didn't like it.

Mummy says we're going to a quiet place. A smaller city than Athens, but with a school, a cinema – the same in every way, but quieter. Fewer people, fewer houses. We're going to Italy because Mummy was born there. And now, now that her husband isn't here any more, we're all going to live there with Mummy's real family. She says we have a big family, a grandmother, lots of aunts and ten cousins. We wonder what they're like.

Mummy's husband isn't our father. But he's Miou's father. Our father was Italian too, but he left Mummy one day to go off with another woman. We were still little. We don't remember anything. He lives far away now. We don't know where. He might have other children. We don't care. We're going to go to a new school with our cousins. We're going buy Rollerblades and get our hair permed. Curly hair is so pretty. Miou has curly hair. It's the only pretty thing about her.

I try to look out of the window without leaning too far forward and knocking Miou off my lap. I can only see the sea from here. Gloomy blue and emerald-green water: the two colour zones alternate but don't mix – they stand out distinct from one another. I think the more water I put between me and that city, the less pain I'll feel. The memories will fly away like the tufts of clouds that trail the plane, after its pointed nose has furrowed smack through the middle of them without the least bit of consideration. Tufts of clouds. Mist.

Mummy is looking out of the window with a preoccupied expression. Miou is dribbling into the collar of Mummy's dress. A slimy, thick thread of spit hangs down and forms a dark pool on the pretty dress Mummy bought especially for her arrival in Italy. It's dark red, with buttons that run down the front all the way to the knee. It's sleeveless and has a pointed shirt collar. Mummy looks pretty in that dress. We said so right away at the shop while she was standing in front of the mirror, smoothing it down over her hips uncertainly. Her serious expression makes us sad. Who knows what she's thinking. She might be sad about leaving Athens. Maybe she's sad about her husband.

We're not. We're not in the least bit sad about him.

Mummy's husband was mean. And ugly, like Miou: all dark and hairy. And he was a liar. Just like Miou, identical.

But Mummy is so beautiful. She looks like us.

Mist that soon dissolves. A blink of the eye and the whole panorama has changed. There's land below us now. A little half-moon-shaped island. Marcella and Giacinta are singing softly in English, some song I've never heard.

I look at them. My two big girls are so beautiful. They're sure of themselves in a way I never was. Will they have a happy life? I ask myself that constantly, and I never know how to answer. I'll try to give them a good life. I've already tried. And considering every-thing, they don't seem sad. They're pretty and vivacious. Their eyes sparkle and they always seem happy. Are they pretending? Or perhaps it's just true that there are people like that, lucky people, whom pain passes over like a pale, fleeting shadow.

When we were in the shoe shop, I couldn't stop staring at their slim calves. Four identical calves carved out of flesh, their sharp little bones fitting perfectly together. They seem fragile, but are solid instead. Their feet are slender, and well formed inside the red shoes; they're like two little girls from a fairy tale, ready to run off to a secret ball in the middle of the night.

I feel Miou's damp breath against my throat. Her spit rolls on to the collar of my dress. I'm getting soaked. I feel incredibly irritated and wish that I didn't. I'd like to be able to accept everything with grace.

But it's so hard.

Mummy is staring at us and there's a kind of smile on her face. It's a tired little smile, it doesn't make her eyes open wider, only her cheekbones stick out.

Who knows what she's seeing.

We like her a lot. She's a good mother. She always says yes, and she listens to us when we want to gossip or complain. Sometimes, she doesn't look like she's there, but she is all the same. She's not one to talk much about things. She'll talk about us, yes, but she never says anything about herself. Maybe grown-ups have to make a special effort when they talk to their children. They're worried about saying the wrong thing.

Miou is crying again. Just as the attendants are about to come through with breakfast. We've never eaten in a plane, but we've seen it on TV. It must be lovely to eat and look out at the clouds.

As long as we don't vomit as soon as we're done.

The attendant pats Miou on the head and ruffles her hair. Miou whirls around, baring her teeth, ready to bite. The stewardess yanks back her hand and we want to laugh but we hold it in.

A dog baby. That's what Miou is. She's just like a dog. One of those ugly, mean little dogs that bark constantly.

The tray is full of things cut into little pieces. A stem of broccoli, slices of salmon and cheese, two white beans, a lettuce leaf, a slice of chocolate cake, bread, a pat of butter in plastic. Endless stuff cut up into doll-sized portions. Miou kicks over Mummy's tray. Everything lands in the middle of the aisle, all over the blue carpet. What an embarrassment. Everyone turns to look at Miou, who's screaming as loud as she can because she hates to be looked at. The attendant cleans up and pretends that everything is all right. Mummy has tears in her eyes but she can't seem to apologise. We keep quiet and keep eating, watching the clouds through the window, like on TV.

I'd like to say something, but the words don't come. Miou just kicked my breakfast tray and everything on it scattered over the carpet. I should apologise to the attendant who is on her knees cleaning up the mess. I should. But I can't do it.

I want to cry. That's all I want.

Miou's behaviour reminds me of her father. He did those kinds of things too. He did them constantly. All it took was for one thing to be out of place when he came home at night and he would throw all the plates off the table and storm out of the house. He was always nervy. And often mean.

But I'm sorry. And to think of him resting now in a city where there's no one left to look after him, it tugs at my heart.

I'm sorry I left, even if I wouldn't go back for anything in the world.

Mummy's husband did that kind of thing too. Like hurling stuff to the ground, or yelling for no reason. We didn't like him. We never liked him. We don't even like him now. Although now at least he can't tell us what to do any more. He's stopped being in command. He's stopped punishing us and Mummy.

The plane swings a little, like it's being blown by a gust of wind. But I might be imagining it.

Marcella and Giacinta have finished eating and seem happy. That's something at least. Miou is crying softly for the moment and I am stroking her neck. I try to get her to eat something. A slow tear slides down my cheek. I'm sorry for Miou. I'm sorry for taking her away from her father.

And I know that it's for ever.

The day Miou started crying we were in the house alone with Mummy's husband. She was out shopping. He was angry about something Mummy had done wrong in the house. He was yelling to himself and banging doors. Then he started on us. He screamed and hit us. Not a lot, but hard. With the flat of his hand he hit us around the head and across our shoulders. He even punched us a couple of times. And he wouldn't stop shouting. We told him that we'd tell Mummy and that he wasn't our father and he couldn't hit us. He said that he was the one who paid the bills and that, father or not, he was the one in charge around the house and that we should do whatever he said. He spoke Greek. Mummy always spoke Italian to us around the house. We talked back to him in Italian. Which made him madder and he started hitting us again. When he stopped, he poured himself an ouzo and took the glass out on to the balcony. He leaned over the railing and watched the lights come on across the city.

We silently stared at him.

Miou was in the corner of the room hugging her doll tight to her chest. She was almost never frightened of her father, except when he yelled. She sat there quietly, her doll in her arms and her eyes wide open.

We looked at each other and it all went very fast.

He put his glass down on the table and leaned a little further over to look at something.

We went towards him.

One of us pushed his shoulders; the other lifted both his feet.

It only lasted a second.

He didn't even scream.

No one saw us. No one but Miou.

We washed the glass and managed to put it away before the people started shouting in the street. Then Miou began to cry. And she hasn't stopped since.

When Mummy came home we kept quiet. What happened? she screamed. Say something! You were here. You must have seen? Did he slip? What happened? Speak to me! She cried loudly and wrung her hands. We were in our room so we didn't hear anything.

The next day Mummy found those papers. They said her husband had a pile of debts and any day they were going to come and take everything away: the house, furniture, the car, everything.

No one asked us any more questions.

Mummy called Italy, she bought tickets, she packed as much as she could. A few days passed.

Now we're flying through the clouds and drinking juice squeezed from Italian blood oranges.

I'm sorry that Miou doesn't have anything of her father's. To remember him by when she's older. And I'm sorry he didn't leave anything, even for her. A note, a goodbye.

It makes me angry to think that he didn't even love her and yet he'd been so insistent about having a baby. I didn't want any more children. Marcella and Giacinta were enough for me. But he said he wanted a baby that was all ours and I gave in. He was my husband after all, even if he did scare me.

I hope that now things will settle down, that the girls will get over it all – Miou too.

And I'm stupid, I'm already thinking I want another man. But I'd like to finally find someone who will take care of me and my girls. The kind of serious man you read about in romantic novels, unlike anyone I've ever met. Though I know such men don't exist.

I'll stay single. I'll take care of myself. And of my babies. My babies. I watch them now in the strange light coming in from outside, a soft golden light that falls across their cheeks in shimmering speckles, as if they were wearing make-up. They're so pretty and good. Despite everything, they have turned out well. And they'll keep on growing, too fast, I'm sure.

There's no more sea below us. There's land and cities. Bologna is still some way off. An hour until we reach the airport where my sister will be waiting for me with her husband and the children. Who knows if they'll be pleased to see us. Who knows if they'll like my girls. Who knows if Miou will stop crying, at least for a while.

There's land under the plane now, and we like to imagine it's a land full of happy children speeding around on Rollerblades. The streets of the cities invaded by boys and girls flying around on skates.

Let's hope that there are good streets for skating in Bologna. Let's hope that Mummy finds work and a new husband. We hope that red shoes aren't silly in Italy. Let's hope that Miou forgets everything and stops crying. Let's hope.

The colour of the ground below is a beautiful green.